THE WHOLE NIGHT
THROUGH

THE WHOLE NIGHT THROUGH

CHRISTIANE FRENETTE

A NOVEL

Translated by Sheila Fischman

Cormorant Books

The publisher gratefully acknowledges the support of the
Canada Council for the Arts and the Ontario Arts Council
for its publishing program. We acknowledge the financial support
of the Government of Canada through the Book Publishing
Industry Development Program (BPIDP) for our publishing activities.

Printed and bound in Canada

NATIONAL LIBRARY OF CANADA CATALOGUING IN PUBLICATION

Frenette, Christiane, 1954–
[Nuit entière. English]
The whole night through : a novel / Christiane Frenette;
translated by Sheila Fischman.

Translation of: La nuit entière.
ISBN 1-896951-59-7

1. Fischman, Sheila II. Title. III. Title: Nuit entière. English.

PS8561.R447N8413 2003   C843'.54   C2003-904233-2

Cover and text design: Tannice Goddard/Soul Oasis Networking
Cover image: Tannice Goddard
Printer: Freisens

CORMORANT BOOKS INC.
215 SPADINA AVENUE, STUDIO 230, TORONTO, ON CANADA M5T 2C7
www.cormorantbooks.com

THE WHOLE NIGHT
THROUGH

*N*ovember. Mid-afternoon. The clouds that have ruled supreme for two days now capitulate. The light seeks an opening, tries to break through. The air is heavy, damp, laden with odours: dead leaves, humus, young conifers. But above all, silence. The silence of a forest road where no one passes. Of a late autumn stripped of its birds. The silence of bare trees.

A clearing. Grass sparse, yellow. Here and there, outcroppings of moss-covered rock. In the background, the edge of the woods, clear as if cut with a knife. A dense barrier. Darkness immediate, decisive. The frontier. Between clearing and road, a white house. Well cared-for. Neither modest nor luxurious. Surprising excrescence here in this place. Near to the house, a garage and an equipment shed in another colour.

A setting in which to inscribe life. A world of forests, of ancient mountains, of winding roads. It always begins with a landscape, a sound, a face, an ache. And the way to abandon oneself to it.

1

*S*he is there, motionless, as if nothing unusual were going on. No tears in her eyes, no rage in her gestures. But for two days now, anguish. She has heated water, poured it into the teapot. Taken a seat by the windows. Next to her, on the small garden table, an open newspaper. The tea's aroma spills onto the freshly painted veranda. The sun finally launches its attack. She opens a window. All the silences melt into one: her own and that of the world.

In the distance, a muffled sound from the forest. Then others, in bursts. To contradict her, to remind her of blazing presences, hidden struggles, secrets revealed, claws plunged into a throat. A moment later, not sounds but a crash rolling, rumbling, coming closer. Furious cracking of branches, clouts on the trees that the moisture in the air spreads as an echo, multiplies. Crows rise, whirl, caw their panic.

And then everything happens very fast. He looms out of the forest. Enormous. His hind legs barely support him. He tries to straighten up, but it's difficult. He advances by fits and starts, powered by his front legs. He drags himself along, turns, makes his way arduously to the middle of the clearing. Abrupt movements of his head make his whole body vibrate, as if he were trying to shake off his antlers. His eyes rolled upwards, his terrified gaze. That moose is going to die before her eyes.

He finally lets go, comes to a halt. In a very slow, resigned movement, he lies down. He gasps, tries to get his breath back. The sound of his respiration fills the space. She goes outside. Crouches at the bottom of the front steps. She isn't afraid. Neither is he. He senses that there is no danger around him. He grows calm, little by little his breathing slows down. They both know that he won't get up again.

Her name is Jeanne, she has lived for a dozen years in a white house in a remote part of eastern North America, where the Appalachians begin. At this precise moment she's alone. A moose is in the process of dying before her eyes.

She won't be able to do anything for him. Will be merely a spectator. His final witness, his first experience of an outsider. He can open the floodgates, she'll gather up everything: the triumph of dawn on the shore of Otter Lake, the taste of twigs, the light touch of females, the trails, exhaustion, solitude, the extreme hunger of March. He can give himself up, she won't betray his secrets. She has learned to be from this place for want of being rooted anywhere else. Will not get the rifle from the cellar. She has no more weight than anything else that surrounds the creature. The sky does not suffer. Thrushes plunge into the forest.

Images shrill in their ears like stray bullets.

FIRST STRAY BULLET

*J*eanne, age nineteen; her worn, baggy sweater. The jam-packed bus. It's hot, there's a bad smell. She feels sick to her stomach. It's the first day of school. Her first class starts in twenty minutes. Philosophy. Nothing interests her.

She doesn't want to be late. She loathes all those eyes focussed on her at once. May as well get this out of the way: she's neither beautiful nor ugly, nor thin nor fat, nor blonde nor brunette. It's a miracle to glimpse her reflection in a mirror.

At night, snug in her bed, Jeanne and her private cinema. She's standing in the middle of an animated crowd that has gathered in a park. Whispers to herself. All at once she raises her voice, oh, hardly at all, just enough to attract attention. Seeing the effect she generates, she speaks louder and louder. The words become light, they lift her up. Jeanne savours the moment. She's floating, the crowd watches her. For a long, long time, until sleep returns her to silence.

Torture. The teacher starts by asking the students to introduce themselves in turn — name, age, place of residence — and what's more, to give their definition of happiness. He lets them have a few minutes to think about it. Without hesitation, on a sheet of paper Jeanne writes the word *sleep*. Because if it's absolutely necessary to find a characteristic for her, it is this: insomniac. From as far back as she can remember, she and sleep have never connected. Already at the age of four or five, she spent long moments awake during the night. She'd understood instinctively that she must not leave herself defenceless, eyes open on the dark. She would switch on the little lamp on her night table and take out the book she'd buried under the covers when she got into bed. Later came books without pictures, it was just a matter of time. Today, it's the images she invents that inhabit her nights. Often during the day, between two classes, she will suddenly fall asleep. Anywhere. The library, the cafeteria, a corridor. As she's not terribly ambitious, it sometimes seems to her that sleep alone would satisfy her hopes.

But obviously she won't explain that sleep equals happiness. In front of her class she prefers grey to colour. If she'd been asked for an answer in writing, then perhaps ...

The teacher signals them to start and points first to a student at the front, on the left. From the centre of the classroom, Jeanne has time to see the answers coming and to amend her own. Each student declares his own grand truth. Five or six answers later, everything has been said. It makes you think that the range of happiness isn't very wide: love, friendship, professional success, family. One brave student suggests money. When her turn comes, her only choice is to join the majority of right-minded individuals. She pronounces, with the detachment of a stone, the word that has come up most often. The train of happiness can chug along without her. Jeanne goes back to float above the crowd that has gathered in the park.

She keeps listening without paying attention. In a very soft and very determined voice, the last student at the back of the room declares quite solemnly: "Marianne, age nineteen, I live at home. Happiness is sleep."

Jeanne takes a nose-dive towards the crowd.

Intrigued, the teacher asks Marianne to clarify her thinking. The young girl explains that sleeping is a subversive act. It means refusing the world as it is and remaking it away from any control. Sleep is the location of an inner revolution.

In the classroom, utter silence. Everyone has turned towards her.

She goes on, talks about Freud and Jung, about the subconscious, the ego, the superego. She flaunts a knowledge

—

that she obviously does not possess. It's not what she says that matters. It's herself. The inflection of her voice, her face at once haughty and sincere. Her motions, fingers pushing back her hair.

Marianne is a snake that dances.

The teacher is speaking again. Jeanne hears his conclusion about happiness but does not understand. She keeps her eyes on Marianne. At the end of the class she picks up this remark: "In short, life boils down to two or three encounters."

The students make their noisy exit. Marianne too, regal. Before she's through the door, the teacher shouts to her: "Good night!"

She responds with a wave and a smile. Jeanne watches, rooted to the spot, incredulous. What has just taken place belongs to her. That notion of happiness and sleep, the way of pronouncing the words, of capturing attention, of floating above the crowd is part of her universe only, of her images. Marianne has reduced to ashes the only place where Jeanne exists. She wishes she hadn't thought that she was the only one who floated above the crowd, that she was the object of everyone's attention, when in fact she was not the one the crowd was watching. Wishes she hadn't seen Marianne floating beside her in all her splendour.

Alone in the classroom, Jeanne gathers up her things. Angry, let down, fascinated. Even in the images she makes up, she can't be more concrete. But be that as it may, something has happened that will change the course of her life, make her thirsty, and bring her to her knees. Perhaps she'll no longer float above the world. Her wings have collapsed, she will smother to death in the midst of the crowd. She'll have to find a way out.

☾

Days pass. Jeanne has no more images in her head. Only Marianne's face, her voice, her torn schoolbag. She looks at horoscopes.

Individuals like Jeanne resemble small animals. They have the survival instinct. Never surrender. Sniff danger. She could go and sit beside Marianne at the back of the classroom, call out to her in the corridors or the cafeteria. But the risk is too great. Her light is so dazzling, it annihilates everything along her way. You don't throw yourself into the lion's jaws without thinking it over. Jeanne does have friends; doesn't spend weekends alone; yesterday she hadn't come home, had slept with François. Gabrielle, the gentle nurse-in-training who also attends the college, is constantly offering her friendship. All of that is called reality, all of that allows her to wait for the small miracle to happen that will make her visible, for the warmth that consumes her to finally pass through the pores of her skin. Jeanne wants to find the key on her own. She's patient. And cautious. Marianne is not the one she's waiting for. Marianne is what happens.

Of course Marianne has noticed this girl who grapples with mirrors. Jeanne won't be her prey or her target. Marianne is generous: she will show her everything that happens once you've found the key. She is the one who speaks to Jeanne first, on their way out of the college. An act that's natural, inevitable. They're in the same philosophy class, after all, thinks Jeanne who hastens to drive the other girl from her mind. But in her bedroom, at two a.m., deep in her usual insomnia, Jeanne, lying on her back, watches Marianne floating. Gently, she approaches Jeanne and speaks to her the way she did as they were leaving the school.

Marianne is looking for the breach that will let her inside. She borrows Jeanne's lecture notes, joins her in the cafeteria at noon, even when François is with her — especially when he's there. She forces her way in. One Friday she slips her phone number into Jeanne's hand.

"Weekends in this town are deadly."

Marianne comes from somewhere else, farther away, bigger. Her parents have separated recently. She didn't choose, she went with her mother. She is the only daughter, she paints, plays the violin, belongs to a theatre company. Jeanne continues to be wary, won't call her. But in a compartment of her wallet she carefully puts the scrap of paper with a number scrawled on it.

Marianne is persistent.

One night Jeanne leaves the door wide open, on purpose. They get together over pizza in a café. Marianne's victory. Beings, things, she needs them. She insists, pesters, carried along by Marianne's incredible charisma. If someone resists, she wages war. Jeanne has just given in. She enters another universe. Life is taking an unexpected turn; all at once she needs that girl so she can inhabit the real world in some other way. Jeanne listens to her talk: the road seems to have been marked, now she just has to walk in the other girl's footsteps and doubts will cancel each other out. There are those who travel in the bright light and don't cast a shadow. Others follow them, watchful, arms held out, palms open. They pick up the crumbs. To them it seems like a lot. Jeanne tries to understand. The words *seduction, charm, influence* escape from her. She loses control, that's new and it's good. For that alone, she would kiss Marianne's feet.

The web is spun gently at first. She drags Jeanne to unfamiliar cafés, into endless fits of laughter, sleepless nights populated with old records. Jeanne follows along with eyes wide open: Marianne attracts looks, weaves her way through individuals, rouses desire, fulfills it sometimes, and goes away once everyone has placed one knee on the ground. Jeanne knows it's not she who exults, but Marianne. Never mind. For the time being, she is experiencing, live, in the daytime, all the images of her nights that have accumulated since she was a child.

François doesn't like Marianne. Calls her "The Diva." Jeanne pretends not to hear. Marianne doesn't like François either.

"Dull," she repeats.

Jeanne feels confusedly that she mustn't give up everything. To keep Marianne's attention, to please her, to be liked by her — that can't be the only truth. She must keep some room, no matter how small, for François, and for the loyalty of several others, including Gabrielle, whom Marianne also loathes because of her discreet but intrusive presence. Jeanne, though, is quite fond of her. In her images, Gabrielle becomes a huge tree with all kinds of roots that surround her, reassuring without stifling. Besides, Gabrielle knows where she comes from — a godforsaken place in the middle of nowhere, somewhere in the mountains, to which she's intensely attached — and knows perfectly well where she's going: to Africa or Asia, to save humanity by administering vaccines and antibiotics.

Jeanne moves between her world and Marianne's, between the sky and the crowd, between her mirrors, which don't send back her reflection, and Marianne's, which shatter every time she walks past them.

☾

Marianne's world fascinates Jeanne, who often goes to her place. Her mother has rented an apartment in an old building in the lower part of town. The walls are covered with paintings and drawings. Everywhere there are books, objects, travel souvenirs, plants. A studied disorder. The place is narrow: their lives seem exposed helter-skelter to the sight of everyone.

Marianne's mother is touchingly attentive to Jeanne, who is amazed every time. She's always smiling and humming. She wears the same clothes as Marianne. Looks ten years younger than her daughter. The two adore one another. Belong to the same race.

Jeanne has also met Marianne's father — an aging, absent-minded adolescent who doesn't want to get old, who spends most of his time travelling the globe as an explorer-tourist.

There again, an indescribable tenderness. Invisible, invincible ties soar between the continents and unite the girl to her father. There's no animosity between Marianne's parents. All three manage to keep the family alive despite the break-up. What touches Jeanne is the love that envelops them even when one of them is absent. They give, take, do not calcu-late, remain standing there, open-armed, come hell or high water.

Hypnotized, Jeanne observes Marianne and her mother. Sometimes, watching simple actions — making a salad in the big Moroccan bowl, cleaning the aquarium, watering the three hibiscus in the living room — she'll leave the room suddenly and rush to the bathroom: there's something unbearable about the special treatment they reserve for one another, that they give to every object they touch. It must be said, it's not at all like that in Jeanne's family. Her own family circle is one in which everyone busies himself to fill the void, to tend their secret wounds. Jeanne has two brothers. They've left home. She lives alone now with her parents. In that family, pleasure is absent and the TV is constantly on. Jeanne has been brought up with reserve: life is neat and tidy. To all appearances. Above all, don't scratch. Every morning as she shuts the door, she heaves a sigh; her house is a house of strangers who speak a language that isn't hers. One day, not all that far off, she will leave them. She smiles.

☾

The school year is ending, the miracle of Marianne lingers on. Jeanne is happy. She'd like it if nothing changed. On one hand, a cozy life with François and Gabrielle. On the other hand, dizziness, fusion, madness. She has ventured farther than she thinks. Jeanne offers Marianne true veneration. One demands. The other complies.

One weekend, Jeanne lets François take her to his parents' cottage. She says nothing about it to Marianne and disappears from Friday till Sunday night. Just a little air, a little distance, to prove to herself that she can walk, that she can laugh without her. Guilty. When she comes back, Marianne is furious and sulks like a child for a week. Jeanne's insomnia turns into nightmares. The images change. There's no crowd in the park now, in fact there's not even a park, only a huge hole in the earth, very deep, a meteorite hole, a hole worthy of the extinction of the dinosaurs. At the bottom of this cold damp hole, Jeanne, naked, curled up in a ball, alone, frightened. Above, the empty, inaccessible sky. She never chooses the scenarios, they materialize without her summoning them. At those times neither the hope of a reconciliation with Marianne, nor the memory of François's warm breath, nor Gabrielle's smile can remove the taste of earth from her mouth and the impression that she's no more than an insect. Jeanne is doubtful: what if everything Marianne revealed to her was false? False generosity, false warmth, a false way of making her chosen ones unique and necessary. Perhaps she puts on a show so she'll receive what she herself can't offer. Marianne wants to be loved, to be adored, because she too is merely a lost insect. And so, next to Jeanne, in the bottom of the hole appears a small phosphorescent larva that tries to devour her. One night, she becomes certain of one thing: that hole isn't meant for her; time is short, she is young; the future — that tyrant — really does exist; trains move along their tracks, planes fly, hands reach out to her — François's and Gabrielle's, for instance; she has a body, a voice; but still, she is no one.

Marianne goes back to hovering around Jeanne. There will be no apology or explanation.

"Want to study for the exam together, Jeanne? You saw how many pages we have to read? We could split it. We could hide out at my place for the weekend. How about it?"

Marianne has slipped her arm into Jeanne's. The hole in the earth closes in, the park reappears and Jeanne gets up, carried away by her friend's impulsiveness.

It's raining. Marianne's mother is away for two days. The girls run the kingdom as they wish. The music is deafening, they've set up their headquarters in the living room. They're flopped on big cushions, notes and textbooks scattered around. They drink very strong coffee. The day goes by, they haven't even said the words "exam" or "study." They laugh.

"Just ten days till school's over," sighs Marianne.

"I have to get a summer job and it isn't easy," says Jeanne.

"I've dealt with that."

"Oh yeah? What?"

"Didn't I tell you?" replies Marianne, surprised.

"No."

"I'm going home to Longueuil, to my father's. I've got a job in a day camp for handicapped kids."

"For the whole summer?"

"Yes, and I don't even know if I'll want to come back."

Uneasiness. Jeanne picks up the coffeepot.

"I'll make more coffee."

Marianne hasn't followed her to the kitchen. Outside, it's raining harder. Jeanne rests her head against a window. Divas are like that. One day or another they get bored. Nothing satisfies them for long. Marianne has already checked out the park. Now she has to float somewhere else, above another crowd.

Jeanne reasons. Life will go on. Yes, it's true, life does go on after earthquakes and tornadoes. It has to be stuck together again. And then one fine day there's nothing left. Just some dates and photos.

Abandonment. That is the name which should be given to the empty feeling that has just assailed her by the window, by the empty coffeepot, the pile of dishes. The rain is pounding on the tin roof of the shed. Marianne has decided to go away. Marianne will go away. Jeanne thinks: "And what if François and Gabrielle leave too?" They'll go at the same time as Marianne. They are a rampart that her departure will tear down. To be abandoned you need to have been surrounded, held on to, you need to have felt the sensation of the other person burning inside you, to have carried her dreams, to have listened to her invent a future that's too wide; you need to have been fed, to have been gorged with all her acts of boldness and her weaknesses. This first abandonment. Jeanne trembles slightly as she pours coffee into the cups.

She comes back to the living room, lets nothing show. Finally Marianne has her nose in a book. She looks up when Jeanne holds out the cup. Marianne is luminous, triumphant. What Jeanne wants is not that she tell her it was just a joke and that never for a minute has she thought about going away; no, Jeanne desires just one thing: to be Marianne. Her hair, her face, her body, her strength, her charm, her cruelty.

Marianne has sensed her distress. At suppertime, she asks if she's hungry. Jeanne says yes, thinks no.

"We'll have a feast to celebrate!" Marianne declares.

"Celebrate what exactly?"

"What do you think? The end of the school year, summer, the fact that the philosophy prof's out of our lives!"

Jeanne would like to add: "And your departure too?" She thinks it might be better, all things considered, to celebrate something that causes pain, that way they'd be more apt to get some chances for feasting in this life.

Marianne orders her to sit down and close her eyes. Jeanne hears her rummaging in the kitchen cupboard.

"Open your eyes! Ta-da!"

Marianne is holding a bottle of champagne. Jeanne has never tasted it. In her head, an image. The worthless painting in her parents' bedroom. A picnic scene. Young women picking flowers, laughing. The faint movement of their dresses. Their carefree existence.

The champagne takes them soaring to an altitude higher than usual. Marianne is jubilant. Jeanne can no longer make out the park and the crowd very clearly, they are hazy little spots waltzing down below. Marianne starts talking about summer plans again. In her voice, such fever, such impatience. Jeanne isn't listening. She is elsewhere, in a place with no name and no colour, a place where she hasn't been since Marianne appeared. A place that has stayed intact. In that spot, very upright, are seated her parents, her brothers, Marianne, François, Gabrielle. Facing them is Jeanne, unmoving, on a round platform that slowly swivels around.

On this moving stage appear and disappear different Jeannes at different ages, dancing and holding out a hand to encourage her to join them. If she doesn't chase that image away she's going to cry. No, not tonight, not in front of Marianne. Too late: the tide rushes in, a powerful wave. She bursts out sobbing.

Marianne stops talking, stunned. This is the first time she's seen Jeanne slip outside herself. She goes on crying. Great sobs lift her shoulders. Wisps of hair stick to her cheeks. On her face, childhood: obstinate, indelible.

Marianne has come closer, puts her arms around Jeanne, asks why she's so upset. It takes Jeanne a while to talk, she can't get one word out. How to express the sensation of being sucked up by the void, how to express the dizziness, the estrangement, the dazzling passage of comets, stars, planets on either side of her body?

"I'm sorry," she finally hiccups, "it must be the champagne."

"Jeanne, Jeanne, don't talk nonsense, not with me. Come on, out with it."

"All those images in my head, it's too much."

"What images?"

Marianne's question is left unanswered. A pause. A silence between them.

They are stretched out on the living-room carpet. Marianne has picked up a heavy wool sweater of her mother's that was lying around and wrapped Jeanne in it. She is holding her and stroking her head.

"What images, what images are you talking about?"

Marianne's voice. Her fingers in Jeanne's hair. Her warmth. And suddenly, this ease at being in the world, surrendered and off guard in someone's arms. To sense the other entering deeply inside herself, wanting only to calm the ocean. To sense the other's strength break the wave, pulverize it, and overwhelm the portion of solitude within her that wants to swallow the universe whole. To feel that she has been saved, multiplied. Everything that she's been waiting for since the meeting between gametes, that she doesn't know how to name, crystallized in this moment. And then slowly, Jeanne tells her: the park, the crowd, the flight, the hole in the earth. The slightest nuances, the most infinitesimal details, textures, odours. Marianne listens, attentive. Hasn't loosened her embrace, hasn't stopped stroking Jeanne's hair. Then Jeanne falls silent. The two girls do not move. The only sound their breathing: one fast and wheezing, the other slow and deep.

Jeanne closes her eyes. A farewell present. Marianne offers her what no one has ever given her. Other arms have opened, but no one has been able to reach her in this way. Not the tender François with his goodwill and his clumsiness; not even her mother when Jeanne was a child, with her deftness and her lack of goodwill. No one. At this moment Marianne asks for nothing in return. Won't ask for Jeanne's body later on, won't claim any pleasure from it. She is simply there with her, warm and alive. Jeanne muses that she's in the process of snatching from the world that which is most mysterious, and she is holding it there, nestled in her hands, in her body.

Eventually she falls asleep in Marianne's arms. Set free. A night without insomnia, without images. A night that no tears will rip open, only the silent cry of cells that are chanting while she sleeps: Present! Present!

☾

The next day, of course, the spell is broken. Marianne's mother comes home. Jeanne has a terrible headache, Marianne is glum, the aftermath of champagne. Jeanne becomes a stranger in the apartment, Marianne does what's needed to let the other know that she's an intruder on the territory. She runs a bath, stays in the bathroom for ages, phones her father while Jeanne, alone, gets rid of the remnants of the night before — dirty dishes, messy living room — as Marianne's mother looks on, amused. She stuffs notes and notebooks into her bag and gets ready to leave without saying goodbye. But the other girl catches up with her at the door.

"Okay, see you at the exam tomorrow!"

Marianne in her bathrobe, hair wrapped in a big white towel, head down, seeming a little guilty at her lack of concern about her friend. Jeanne's absolution.

"Right, see you tomorrow."

☾

Their official story ends here. On this dark wood staircase that Jeanne descends, a hellish pounding at her temples every time she sets foot on a step. It's there in the streets she walks along on this grey Sunday in springtime, that she first feels time accelerating in her bones, her muscles, her skin. Jeanne hears herself growing old. What remains of childhood is abandoning her.

One tiny thing, a ridiculous drama, not even a broken heart or a bereavement. Just the victory of images over reality; from now on the only place where Jeanne will be able to hide Marianne.

Between them, finally, Jeanne has to acknowledge, nothing really happened. You couldn't talk about grand feelings or about deep ties that have endured since childhood. Marianne had appeared at the beginning of a school year, had shown Jeanne that it was possible to exist, fully, openly, at every second. But above all, that it was possible to embrace. And as the earth turns, Marianne was about to disappear. They were simply two young women at the threshold of their lives, and their only baggage was their nineteen years. Marianne was endowed with a knowledge that Jeanne did not possess, she had flashed across her life like lightning and had let her catch a glimpse of the cave, the key, the treasure. Now Jeanne just had to get moving, to cross the sea, to climb Everest, and finally, hardest of all, to find the right cave.

Jeanne in Marianne's arms: already an image imprinted on her body. Weeks, months of lightness and laughter, reduced to one very small, obvious fact: we never have enough, we never do enough. In love as in everything else.

((

Final week of school. Jeanne is swept up in the whirlwind of exams and assignments to hand in. At the college, when she runs into Marianne, who wants to make contact, Jeanne pleads overwork: a fragile defence against Marianne's departure. Marianne doesn't push it because everything has been said. The rest of the work that's gone into forging the relationship between them will finish unravelling slowly, nearly imperceptibly, over the few days when they meet again. Jeanne will remember the lesson. No matter what the expedition is, you always come back down the mountain that you've climbed dazzled and euphoric from the heights.

Now Jeanne has finished her last exam. She's relieved. She'll have to find a job, another rhythm; she'll don a different skin from that of the discreet student in which she now feels cramped. She expects nothing from these few months, nothing but the sun on her skin, the taste of peaches, and her bedroom window wide open onto the warm night.

Jeanne goes down to the locker room. She has to empty hers. In front of another one, half-open, she stops. Marianne has already been and gone. At the back, some crumpled papers. Jeanne unfolds them one by one, warily, constantly looking around for fear that Marianne will suddenly appear and rebuke her for barging into her life.

Jeanne shuttles back and forth between her locker and the trash can at the end of the row. Nietzsche, Baudelaire, the *Refus global* manifesto, Precambrian civilizations — it all goes in. The teachers are always advising them to hold on to everything, not get rid of anything they've learned in school. She disobeys, takes a certain pleasure in doing so. What possible use is the truth according to all these oddballs, she wonders, when it's so hard to find your own?

Behind her, a voice.

"Jeanne, at last!"

It's Gabrielle, out of breath, smiling as usual.

"I've been running after you for an hour! I'm going home

tonight. I didn't want to leave without saying goodbye."

Jeanne, uncomfortable, doesn't know what to say. During the year she'd neglected Gabrielle even while keeping her close, busy as she was in the court of Marianne. But Gabrielle doesn't demand exclusivity. She is of the race of those who understand that you mustn't expect anything from others, that humanity is indivisible: she wants to embrace the entire world. Whether your name is François, Jeanne, or Marianne, it's all the same. She refuses to make distinctions. There are billions of similar humans, she would love them all. In the time when God still existed, Gabrielle would have been a saint.

"Let's go have a beer!"

"I have to finish cleaning out this locker."

While saying these words, Jeanne weighs the importance of their farewells to Gabrielle.

"Oh well, why not!"

She grabs whatever is left and goes straight to the trash can.

In the pub across from the college are the final crowds before the summer calm, the dead season. There are no tables free so they're sitting at the bar. Gabrielle is excited.

"I've finished school! I'm a nurse! At last I can do the work I wanted. You see, we don't just move forward, in the end we arrive somewhere."

She'd like to start working as soon as possible, to acquire

enough experience so that her candidature as an aid worker will be taken seriously.

"I want to travel, get to know all sorts of different human beings, especially the destitute. I want to be useful, not be satisfied with the easy life. And I can't wait!"

Gabrielle has hopes and dreams. Vast, enveloping, like her smile. Jeanne could have paid closer attention: are dreams contagious? Gabrielle and Marianne have something in common, she thinks. Each has found her breathing space, a way to spread her wings. And healing or seduction are approaches to life that are just as worthy as others. At least they've found one.

Before she leaves Jeanne, Gabrielle takes from her bag a photocopy on which she's written her address and phone number, and drawn a road map to her house.

"I'll be there till I get a job. And when I've left for the end of the world, my parents will know how to get in touch."

She laughs heartily, snapping her fingers as if the future would instantaneously answer her call and lie down at her feet like a loyal and well-trained dog.

Jeanne looks at the hand-drawn map.

"That's a long way from here!"

"Practically at the American border. In the Appalachians."

"What's it like there?"

"Woods, woods, woods. But farming too. Peaceful. I don't think Marianne would like it."

Gabrielle has spoken her name, has registered the difference between them.

Jeanne smiles. Too late for friendship today. But Gabrielle's enthusiasm overwhelms her. When they part on the sidewalk, it's Jeanne who initiates a hug. As she expresses the wish that all Gabrielle's dreams will come true, she hears Marianne's voice burst from her throat.

☾

After Marianne and Gabrielle there's only François to erase. She can't help it that she has this need to wash away everything, to wipe the slate clean. Without sadness. She is standing with him in the middle of a photo, the pose sweet and friendly. But still. And now is the time for movement: hasn't she been a sherpa during all these months? Didn't she carry Marianne's baggage, pitch the tent, and lay the fire for her when evening came? Now Jeanne is well acquainted with the trails, the traps, the stopping places. "Yes," she tells herself on her way to François's place, "by myself, all by myself."

Later that evening, when Jeanne dons kid gloves and murmurs "the end," when she sees François go pale and get lost in the fog, when she answers his incredulous why's, she senses again Marianne's voice speaking for her. It's not Marianne who comes looking for her, it's Jeanne who goes in search of Marianne on the other side of abandonment.

She goes home late, along deserted streets. The solitary walk begins right here, where faces disappear, and places. Marianne's outbursts, Gabrielle's smile, François's dismay just now: Jeanne has put them all together, tied them up in a package and dropped it off on a corner. Others will find them, will divide them up for their happiness or their grief, perhaps they'll learn of Jeanne's existence in the course of a remark or a childhood memory. In the end we are nothing more than the detail in a painting, an innocuous, silent form among so many others, floating above a park or a life.

Darkness, the sound of the wind in the leaves. "Tonight, no insomnia. I'm going to sleep, sleep till noon tomorrow. When I wake up, my dreams will be new, they'll never have been dreamed by anyone else."

On her bed, an envelope. Next to it a note jotted by her mother: "Your friend came to say goodbye before she left." Jeanne missed the last rendezvous. Oh well, it doesn't matter now, she thinks as she opens the envelope. No letter. But the necklace of blue beads that Marianne claimed was so

—

precious, from which she was never parted. A travel souvenir from her father. From Nepal. Marianne the virtuoso. A blue necklace for the loyal sherpa.

2

He hasn't moved for an hour. The light is fading. Now and then he raises his head and breathes the air as if it were the last time. It's cold. Jeanne gets up carefully and leaves her lookout for a few moments to fetch binoculars and a warmer coat. The moose doesn't move a muscle. She could swear that his eyes are pleading with her not to leave him alone. When she comes back she sits on the same step, in the same position. Through the binoculars she examines him; there's a wound on his back, at the base of the withers. A mixture of dried blood and fresh. A bullet or an arrow, immediate pain, the strength to run away, the trail lost by the hunter, the pain worse and worse, panic — and now the end, here, in the clearing. Or simply old age, back grazed by a sharp branch and by the refusal to submit.

The last rays of daylight on the animal. All around, the forest holds its breath. The colours are fading, running together. The hour — when one is alone — when one must surrender everything to the night: smells, sounds, the fear of living and the fear of dying. Jeanne doesn't take her eyes off him. Until darkness separates them for good and closes each of them inside his own images, his own peril.

In life, nothing happens without a reason. There's no such thing as chance, Jeanne thinks, as she places her hand on her neck, on the blue bead necklace. The old cliché. It was Marianne's motto when things slipped from her hands and she was trying to bring them back. Marianne. Six thousand, eight hundred and nine days separate them. Jeanne keeps track, and she wears the necklace. We can't choose who we are, so we choose who we want to be. Everest and blue necklaces exist to mark the way.

Marianne, Marianne, where is she right now? Jeanne wonders. In a while she'll walk into some bar that's all the rage, exhausted but radiant, she's had such a good day: she'll have talked some recalcitrant investors into buying paintings, into pumping more money into a film production, into putting on a play with a cast of twenty. They'll have listened for hours, she will have overcome all their resistance. She'll have handled the figures, the profits, the fallout, like a juggler. She will know that it wasn't her skill that acted in her favour:

it was the scent of Samsara on her skin, her long black hair, so shiny, her eyes that pierce the soul. They'll sign because of her charm. She'll go off and join friends, wear a designer suit, jewels, she'll talk loudly. She'll be offered a martini. She'll light a cigarette, her hand on the hand of the man who holds the lighter.

For eighteen years, Jeanne has created Marianne's life day by day.

Because when she entered her own story, she couldn't reconcile herself to killing her old images. She had mastered them and directed them towards Marianne. Who sometimes replied to Jeanne, cleared the path for her to follow, showed her how to open her arms to the distress of another, how to attract love to herself. At such times, Jeanne savoured a small victory: she had made Marianne her sherpa. Never for long, though. During steep climbs it was Marianne who headed the expedition, with Jeanne following, weighed down enough for two.

The moose moans. Spasms shake him. The rifle in the cellar. Should she finish him off? Jeanne wonders. Settle scores with him as if he'd committed a crime?

A flight of wild ducks flies above the clearing. The escape to the south. Another way to survive. Their anxious cries with every stroke of a wing. Courage and faith along the way.

Jeanne thinks about her son. At this time of day he is walking down the main street of the village, dawdling. His cap is pulled so far down on his head you can see only half of his face. He's hungry.

This is also the time when, every day, at the other end of the street, the baker places in his window the notice: Open Tomorrow. This is the time when, in the back of the shop, he rests his head against the wall and counts the empty hours till dawn, till the moment when he will plunge his hands back into the flour.

SECOND STRAY BULLET

$\mathcal{J}$eanne turns over and over in her fingers a blue-bordered ivory business card. Her name is there for all to see, and just below it, her occupation: translator. She's just landed her first job, some informative brochures about the performance of some stocks for a firm of financial advisors. Don't look a gift horse in the mouth. Jeanne is twenty-four years old. She spent a long time in school, cared passionately about her studies. She specialized in literary translation, which fits what she is, matches her innate attraction to unknown worlds. Translation, it seems to her, means stepping into someone's room while he sleeps and then, with infinite care, giving a new appearance to everything that is part of that world, without distorting its essence. Work that is like fine surgery, like goldsmithing; and then once it is finished, a new life, a new book. She doesn't change. Shadows always interest her more than the light, as long as she doesn't stray too far away from it.

She lives alone, in a small furnished apartment. Works weekends as a cook in an Italian restaurant. To keep body and

---

soul together. Hasn't solved her insomnia problem. She has however become more self-confident. Mirrors now send back her reflection. For a long time she missed Marianne. Jeanne occupies a space that suits her, she moves about, discreet but present, organizes her life like a book to be translated: first the general idea, the atmosphere, then the chapter, the page, the paragraph, the sentence, the word. Each hardship, each joy taking part in another, larger one, and finally the whole thing, upright and orderly.

She did try after Marianne went away to tangle up her life. Just to see. To play a role, to work out a character for herself. Inside her Marianne's voice whispered: "You're making yourself look ridiculous!" So then she went back to her tame acquaintances, her dark clothes, put on her own skin again.

Jeanne has made new friends. Individuals who resemble her, most of them met when she was studying translation. With them she has learned to speak out, to stand up for her convictions. How to render a poem without betraying it? In translation, the proper balance is sometimes determined by just one word. Poorly chosen, it can make the original text insignificant. Whole nights spent debating.

Jeanne has become an avid cyclist again. For financial reasons, initially. When she left her father's house with her only baggage a suitcase and two green garbage bags, she took her old bike so she wouldn't have to spend a cent on public transportation. During the months when snow doesn't prevent her from riding, she saves enough to pay for part of her groceries. While she was in school, whenever she stumbled over something that was hard to translate, she'd memorize it, hop on her bike, and ride until the words revealed themselves without betrayal. Then come home triumphant and exhausted. For her twenty-second birthday she got a state-of-the-art mountain bike. Jeanne had read somewhere that exercise helps one to sleep. She became even more fervent, threw herself frenetically into cycling. She has pedalled so much since that if the article was right, she'd no longer be insomniac but would live in a permanently comatose state.

Her sleepless nights were sometimes spent in Marianne's company. A matter of keeping up to date. She must have finished her education too. Jeanne places her in the centre of images where life is easy, where Marianne continues to dance in the light. Most often, though, it's other images that creep into her insomnia. Always the same ones: arms embracing warm bodies, hands slowly stroking hair. Images which say that everything is experienced only once, that afterwards there are no more discoveries, only an obsession with those arms at every heartbeat. A turmoil of images that translating the most beautiful piece of writing in the world or cycling across North America would be unable to quell.

It didn't take Jeanne long to translate the brochures about share prices. She received a cheque in the mail. She's gone back to looking for work, which she hates. So Saturdays and Sundays, when she dons her cook's apron, life seems exquisitely simple. For her, the culinary art is to her hands what translation is to her head. Work that requires at once precision and invention, aromas and textures. The chef is Italian. Jeanne has promised herself that this is where she'll study a third language. And no one should be surprised, on entering the kitchen, to see on the slate not the day's menu, but verb conjugations and words that are hard to spell. When she reminds herself that she's working in this bistro out of necessity, she's well aware that her need is not merely financial. The excitement of Saturday night, when the restaurant is packed — the tongue-lashings over a forgotten order, the Rossini arias sung by the chef, the kitchen to clean and the dishes to wash at one in the morning, and finally, the cigarette and the glass of Chianti at three, when the employees can finally catch their breath before they go to sleep — all that, translation will never offer her.

Weekends, Jeanne works long hours. Though she finishes very late at night, she opens the bistro on Sunday morning. For her, it is a moment of grace to be alone in the kitchen, absolute ruler over fried eggs and fruit crêpes. The restaurant has few customers for breakfast. Sometimes she realizes with concern that this work is more fulfilling than translation. Is that normal? she wonders. What would happen if one day Marianne should walk into the bistro and see her decked out in her Italian sous-chef's outfit? Would she blush with shame or greet her proudly with "Buon giorno"?

☾

Jeanne wants to do something extravagant with the cheque for her first translation. A senseless expenditure of a reasonable sum. In the biggest mall in town she spends an entire afternoon looking for something wild, something useless. Without success. She doesn't possess the art of squandering money. After a few hours, furious at having wasted her time, she decides to go home. And just as she gets to the main doors and is releasing her bike from the stand, a young woman comes up to her and says her name. A young woman her age, very thin, who is walking with a cane; a young woman with frightened eyes, with features paradoxically gentle and strained, whose every move, every muscle betrays effort and discomfort.

For a few moments, Jeanne is bewildered. Her memory has to peel away one by one the new skins that have transformed Gabrielle.

"Jeanne!"

"Gabrielle!"

She is accompanied by her parents, who stay in the background. Their smiles, similar to their daughter's. The two young women begin by praising chance, then count the years that have separated them. They haven't tried to get together. Gabrielle speaks slowly, with effort. On the left side of her face, small involuntary movements of the muscles give her a fragility that's new to Jeanne.

One can't ask Gabrielle: "What have you been up to?" Go back instead to the past, to the moment when things toppled over.

"What happened to you?" Jeanne dares to ask.

"An accident. A car."

"A long time ago?"

"Nearly five years now. Actually, a few weeks after I finished school."

Jeanne realizes that Gabrielle has not become a nurse, has never taken off to save humanity.

Gabrielle questions her in turn. Jeanne talks about Italian cooking and the share price brochures. Then, as if they've already exhausted the essentials, Gabrielle turns towards her parents who are waiting for her.

"Well, I have to go now."

"Remember," says Jeanne to keep her there, "that map you gave me for getting to your place? I still have it. Is it still good?"

In Gabrielle's eyes, a supplication, a plea.

"Yes."

On her lips, her old smile.

Jeanne, rooted there, one hand holding on to her bike, watches her go away flanked by her parents. Jeanne had always thought that one day she would step into life through the front door. That all the knowledge she would take in, all her efforts, small and large, to be visible, had as their only goal the widening of that doorway. Often she saw herself walking through it for good, certain she'd be warned in advance. Her adolescent images were of storms, wind, cliffs overhanging the sea, Beethoven symphonies and she herself, arms flung wide, finally taking her place at the exact centre of the world, exclaiming, "Here I am!" Yes, she was right. She's been warned. But the scenario now presents itself in a manner radically different from her adolescent fantasies. Before her, there is no wide-open door, no riotous nature, no music. Only hundreds of vehicles lined up in a vast parking lot, only the metallic glimmer of their colours in the compelling sunlight, only this spring afternoon, abnormally warm for the season, only the noise from the fast lane and the city's profile on the horizon, only that young woman who limps and turns in her direction one last time, and waves.

☾

Jeanne has to first board a bus that will take an hour to carry her to a small town on the St. Lawrence. When she gets on, nearly all the seats are occupied by people going much farther than she is. Sitting at the back, on the aisle, she holds a grocery bag and worries that the fresh pasta and the caper sauce inside won't withstand the heat. Actually, she's worried because she thinks that she herself is inappropriate, with her pasta, her good health, her body in perfect running order. And what if the comparison is unbearable to Gabrielle? She would have preferred to come on her bike — which would no doubt have relieved her discomfort — but it's too far to where she's going and her boss expects her at the restaurant on Saturday morning.

Gabrielle might be disappointed if Jeanne is insensitive to the countryside she's travelling through on the way to see her. For the time being, all it has to offer is two grey strips separated by the median or by trees. Sometimes the river appears in the distance as an extension of the sky, as a victory over the ordinary.

In the second bus there are just four passengers. Seated symmetrically, two in front, two in the middle, one on either side. The fabric on the seats is worn. The vehicle, an old model, moves slowly. It couldn't go very fast in any case, because they aren't on a highway now but on a rather narrow road that runs into the back country. Jeanne records conscientiously everything she sees. First the plain and its abundance: silos, barns, charming little houses arranged geo-metrically in space. Then, gradually, islands of forests, rocks, and trees along the fences, more modest houses, life a little harder. The bus stops in each of the villages. The driver delivers parcels, leaves them off at service stations or grocery stores.

The back country. Villages more and more sporadic. A world of wood, of dips and heights. Gabrielle's country. So far away, so strange, yet it's been only two hours since she started out.

She is the last passenger off the bus. A godforsaken village on the flank of the mountain, densely surrounded by forest. A main street, a few cross streets going nowhere or turning into forest roads, the church, a post office. And a bakery right out of the nineteenth century, white, spotless.

"Welcome to the end of the world!"

Gabrielle links arms with Jeanne. They walk slowly. She tells her about the village. In her haste, the words all rush together and for a few moments she loses the thread of her thoughts. During these brief pauses, Marianne's voice — again, always — in Jeanne: "Would you mind telling me what the hell you're doing here?" For once, Marianne will have to get along without an answer.

Gabrielle's parents are happy Jeanne has come to visit. As if she had the power to break up time, to take the calendar back to the proper dates, before the darkness in their daughter's body. Who finally smiles, laughs heartily when Jeanne lists for her suspicious father the ingredients in the Italian caper sauce she's just given them. Their house, set back from the street a little, is one of the last in the tight nucleus that makes up the village. Through the windows on one side, a full view of the houses in a neat row along the street, and on the other side, the mountain, the road that slips away, the sky, its carefree silence, and its jumble of clouds.

Jeanne is given the big bedroom upstairs, next to Gabrielle's. Everything in this house is excessively clean and shiny. In the bathroom that the two young women share, on the shelf by the mirror are the bottles of Gabrielle's pills; numerous, desperately numerous. She'll have to tell me all about it, thinks Jeanne. And because their close friendship has been revived now, easily, because for Gabrielle speaking is the only activity that doesn't exhaust her body, Jeanne asks the question after supper, when they're sitting in the big swing, watching the light run aground on the mountain.

"I'll tell you, but I don't remember much. They figure it happened very quickly, in a few minutes, a few crucial seconds. It was just after midnight, I was on my way home. It was hot, a very hot night in July. I'd spent the evening in a bar in the next village, with my cousins. I hadn't been drinking. I was driving my father's car. I had a flat. I didn't know how to change the tire. Up till then, I remember everything. I had to wait a long time till someone came along; during the week the road is deserted at night. I may have walked for a while. Then a car hit me and threw me head first into a tree. And kept driving. Back home, my mother got worried and called my cousins, and right after that my father and my brother went out to look for me. When they found me at the side of the road, I'd already been there for a while. I emerged from the coma a few days later. I had a fractured skull, some broken bones. Months of immobilization, months of rehab, neurological damage, not to mention the fact that now I'm afraid of my shadow, I have pains in my bones and muscles, I'm overwhelmed by anxiety over nothing. And no way out, not even an emergency exit."

Gabrielle told it all in one breath, without hesitation, for once.

"And the person who hit you?"

"We never knew who it was."

"Would you have wanted him to be found?"

"You'll think I'm ridiculous, but at first it didn't occur to me. All I could see when I tried to recreate the accident was the tree I crashed into. As if it was the guilty party … See, a few centimetres to the left and I'd have landed on a carpet of leaves. And everything might have been different. But later on, sure, I would've liked him to be found and forced to pay. Not now, though. I still feel this resentment, this bitterness, it's hard to explain. It isn't rage or a thirst for revenge. That's not what I want. It's rough, feeling that kind of resentment. I leave it to others."

"Who? Your parents seem totally at peace with life."

"Well, my brother."

"Your brother?"

"Wait till you see him — he's something else. You'll understand why I talk about rage."

☾

In the middle of the night Jeanne, of course, isn't asleep. The window and the curtains are open. She's amazed at how dark the night is. And at the silence. She doesn't call to Marianne, doesn't try to place herself inside a reassuring image. She is with Gabrielle, who's asleep on the other side of the wall, who may right now be dreaming about what she might have become. Jeanne feels submerged under what she calls her wave of uselessness: translation, Italian cooking, her bike, her little quirks: already, at twenty-four, her industrious per-severance and, above all, the naïveté that makes her believe she's going somewhere. While Gabrielle, standing on her ice floe, watches the shore move away, very aware that no one will save her.

Gabrielle is awake; Jeanne pricks up her ear. Listens to her friend's clumsiness: the cane hitting the floor, a chair overturned. In the bathroom, the sound of water. Then some pill bottles fall off the shelf, a glass shatters on the tile floor.

Jeanne jumps up. Gabrielle is huddled on the edge of the bathtub, sweating.

"Careful! Don't come in, you'll cut yourself."

She is trembling, breathing hard. Jeanne doesn't listen, goes to her.

"Is something wrong? Are you in pain?"

"It isn't serious, it happens sometimes. I wake with a start and I panic. The first few times it was hell. I didn't know what to do. But I do now. I just took a pill. In a few minutes I'll be fine."

"Did you have a nightmare? Were you reliving the accident?"

"I don't relive anything, I don't live, that's the difference, that's what upsets me. I don't have a life, Jeanne, not behind me and not ahead of me, all I have is a series of days marked by fatigue, pain, anxiety. No plans, no dreams. Inside my head everything has changed, I can't control my fear. My body has let me down. Some days the pain is so bad it makes me so dizzy that I can't get out of bed. I'm dependent on everybody. I'm nothing."

Jeanne doesn't know how to react. She thinks, Marianne is never there when I need her. She can't think of anything more intelligent to do than pick up the shards of glass on the floor.

They go back to Gabrielle's room when she starts to feel the effect of the pill. Jeanne tucks her in and sits beside her.

"You'll end up knowing everything about me!"

She's calm now. Jeanne takes her hand.

—

"I'll stay with you till you fall asleep."

Gabrielle closes her eyes, surrenders herself completely.

"You see, it isn't that complicated after all." And Marianne chortles in Jeanne's ear.

In the morning, Gabrielle is still asleep when Jeanne goes downstairs.

"Gabrielle had a panic attack, didn't she?" her mother asks apologetically. "When I realized you'd got up I didn't go upstairs. It's good for her to open up to someone besides us. I hope it wasn't too disturbing for you."

"Not at all," Jeanne assures her, "I just wish I could have done something for her …"

She doesn't complete her sentence. Uncomfortable, they both fall silent: helplessness doesn't need words.

"You've brought the good weather," says Gabrielle's mother, changing the subject.

"Can I do something to help?" Jeanne replies, as if to thank her.

"As a matter of fact, yes. Why not take advantage of the sun? We're out of bread. Would you go and get some at the bakery?"

Jeanne shuts the door behind her, sets off down the main street. Feels as if she's been doing this forever. She turns her head to look at Gabrielle's window. Strangely enough the world is in order. Herself, in the middle, and nothing seems more important than the pale young woman up there in her bed; than the green of the mountain; than the impudent and laughing morning light on the village. Jeanne has found something. She doesn't really know what it is that she's found on her way to buy bread. An ease she hasn't known before, the confidence that she hasn't made a mistake.

3

Moose, Jeanne has often seen up close. Now and then one appears on the edge of the woods at dawn or at sunset. These animals are only passing by, the forest calls them back at once. One day the scene had been fabulous: a female had ventured into the clearing, attracted by the hay, though there wasn't much. Was followed a few moments later by two fearful, fragile, long-legged calves. They'd fed themselves for long minutes in absolute peace. They came nowhere near the house. Jeanne had observed them in silence, holding her newborn son in her arms. The tremendous responsibility for the life of a person other than herself was something she'd felt for the first time in front of that animal and her young. Beyond the individuals who'd held her back, there had been those animal presences, nature that was submissive to man's traps and the fury of the climate, and above all the deceptive immutability of this universe in which every living form, without distinction, is subject to implacable laws of survival.

With the end of daylight, the dampness has intensified and Jeanne feels colder and colder. When the darkness is complete she'll go inside for a while to get warm. Then she will take up her position on the veranda. She'll open the windows to hear if the moose is moving or if it's gasping again.

Jeanne is fascinated by the habits of moose. The females stay with their young from one calving till the next. The oldest yield their places to the newborn. The females are never alone. It's in the nature of things, she thinks. But the males are constantly wandering on their own. Sometimes in winter they group together. Two or three individuals in a feeding place. Only then. Plus the few weeks in autumn with the females, for the unstoppable continuation of life. The rest of the time they are alone, in the silence and the din of the world.

Jeanne's mind is wandering. What if she were in the moose's place? If, for instance, she got burned, fell, injured herself — who would rescue her? The house is isolated, no one would know. What if she lacked the strength to drag herself to the phone? Even if she could with tremendous difficulty dial a number, whom would she call? At the other end of the line the carefree voice of a very young woman, no more than twenty years old: Marianne. Jeanne would hang up immediately. "You couldn't save me if that was how things were." Marianne's face, a little sad, a little angry, becomes slowly blurred in the dim light at the edge of the woods.

Who would save her? Gabrielle? No. She isn't strong enough. And Jeanne needs her in a different way. Needs her smile, her hands on the shoulders of the son they share. No, Gabrielle would be ready to do anything to help her, but it isn't possible.

Paul. By instinct, it's to him that she would turn. But she wouldn't know how to reach him at this point. He left yesterday, as he does every time his anger devastates him. He understood long ago that it was better to burn off his anger elsewhere than to drag Jeanne along with him.

She would have just one number to call. He would come right away. Covered in flour. He'd know everything to be done or not done. He'd know what to do about the blood or the burned skin. He'd say something silly to make her laugh. And it would work. She'd laugh and her ribs would be terribly sore. She would be saved.

Finally, Jeanne would call the nearest neighbour and all would end well. Those who save you are never the ones you think. The wave rises, a dizziness identical to the one that preceded Marianne's departure grabs her by the throat. Before her, the animal. Both of them mute, motionless. Alone and together. She lets the images come, images of her arms closing around someone who had ordered her: "Stay!" And who's not there now to preserve the light from the ascendancy of darkness, the moose from death, and Jeanne herself from the bullet that she took right in the chest, yesterday, at that same hour.

THIRD STRAY BULLET

*T*he captivating aroma of freshly baked bread, the only indication that the place is a bakery, spreads to the outside. The solid wood building, white as flour, is built in a remarkable architectural style that contrasts sharply with the houses in the village. Jeanne pushes open the door, there's a tinkling of little bells; the dark premises are lit by a few floury windows that block the light. At the front, the retail sales counter. The loaves sit on adjustable metal racks. Here and there, where everyone can see them, bread tins in different sizes and shapes. At the back, a wide opening into the room where the dough is kneaded and the bread baked. She doesn't see anyone, but that room is where the work is going on. She waits, no one comes. A moment later, Victor, the baker, notices her.

"You should have warned me!" he says dryly.

He likes it when unknown faces appear in his bakery.

"I've never been here before!" retorts Jeanne.

And that was how, through words, they met and, more important, recognized one another. He, the outsider in the village, though he came here thirty years ago as a child; he who has chosen to live away from everyone, whom the others would tend to distrust if he didn't make the best bread you could find. And she, who doesn't know by what miracle people, things, the countryside here have immediately adopted her and have become so familiar in less than twenty-four hours.

Facing her, motionless, hands on hips, Victor doesn't ask where she's from or what she's doing there. She is the one who asks questions. About the bread, about the bakery trade. He takes her into the back, shows her around, explains. Bread is Victor's first passion. He hands Jeanne an apron so she can take the last batch from the oven with him. When it's done, he says: "I imagine you wanted some bread?"

She realizes that Gabrielle's mother didn't mention what kind she wanted or how much to buy.

"I don't know exactly what to get."

"Who's it for?"

"The Germains."

He takes some loaves from the rack, bags them. Just before Jeanne leaves, Victor leans across to her.

"I need an aide-de-camp for the summer!"

☾

She takes her time going home. It's nearly noon when she arrives back at the house. The table is set. Gabrielle is sitting in the rocker. Looking drawn. In pain. This isn't a good day.

All the same, she smiles. A frail little smile, forced. Her father, kidding her, feigns impatience in front of Jeanne.

"How's the bread? Still fresh?"

They've started to eat when the sound of a car door makes the parents turn and look out the window. Gabrielle warns Jeanne: "Here comes the rest of the family."

The door opens abruptly. He often shows up without warning, noon or night, at mealtime. He lives alone several kilometres from the village. Hefty, older than his sister. She's right when she refers to him as a rebel. What is striking at first glance, on his face, in his movements, is his expression, at once closed and exasperated. He comes in, barely says hello, heads for the sink, but his mother stops him, introduces them: "A friend of Gabrielle's."

He is obviously surprised. For five years now Gabrielle has been living as a recluse. He takes a plate and cutlery from the cupboard and sits down across from Jeanne. He asks his sister how she is. The conversation involves him, Gabrielle, and their parents. Jeanne doesn't take part. Ill at ease, suddenly small, an outsider. Now and then Paul steals a glance at her, furtive, severe, as if to make sure that she won't run away. She's taken back years, to a classroom. The first meeting with Marianne. Paul's ability to attract attention, his need for exclusive rights, his drawling voice, his way of breaking off bread with his hands and offering some to Gabrielle — I'm protecting you, he seems to be telling her — his parents' admiring attitude, his charisma, his power to attract. Like Marianne, minus her kindness. Jeanne on the verge of a relapse, as if one never grows up, never learns.

"What did you think of Victor?"

Gabrielle's mother brings Jeanne back into their world. In her question, a great deal of curiosity. Victor, the master of bread, the dropout, the docile and unassuming black sheep. Seen from a different angle, Victor is interesting.

Jeanne describes her encounter with the baker in detail. The words are unknotted, she's comfortable again. The four others listen, surprised. Usually Victor is neither friendly nor pleasant with customers or anyone else. Shows only a polite and docile reserve. Gabrielle makes joking comments on her friend's remarks. She laughs. Jeanne lays it on because it's the only thing that matters: to draw Gabrielle's laughter from her body, her distress, her pain. And Paul, impassive, understands what she's up to. Since the accident it's become so rare to see Gabrielle joking, mocking. Like before. His gaze lands on Jeanne and stays there. Determined to discover the illusion and the mechanisms behind her action. When she tells them that Victor wants to hire her for the summer, they're astounded. Not since he took over the bakery, and even in his grandfather's day, has anyone set foot inside except as a customer.

She hasn't told them everything about her meeting with Victor. How to explain that in the middle of a steep trail, when the air becomes icy and they assess their isolation, exhausted, sherpas send out muffled cries to one another: an appeal, a way of saying, We don't know why we have to climb, but we're together.

The account of her visit to the bakery has had its effect. Jeanne enjoys it. A little exhilaration. At the end of the meal when Paul, before he leaves, finally brings himself to speak to her directly and asks if she intends to stay here for long, she could swear that he made a mistake and called her Marianne.

☾

Gabrielle has gone to bed early, exhausted. Jeanne is sitting up in bed, chin resting on her knees. Another night waiting for sleep. She spent the evening with Gabrielle's parents. They talked about themselves, about their children, their concerns about getting old. Who would look after their daughter? She had come to them late. They were in their forties. Paul was ten when she was born. They weren't expecting her. They had long since resigned themselves to having just the one child. Gabrielle entered their lives like the sun. A talkative, cheerful girl. The absolute antithesis to Paul, whose childhood got away from them, so marked had it been by gusts and squalls. They'd been afraid that he would reject her, but, against all expectations, he's been devoted to her. While Gabrielle hadn't been able to disarm him, she was able to show him that there existed a solution through affection, where he could take refuge when he wanted but, above all, when he was able. They're convinced that without Gabrielle, Paul would have turned out badly because he'd have had only his rage to hold on to. She had known how to flush out what they hadn't guessed at in him: the hidden, narrow road on which love travels, in secret and sheltered from the blows and threats of anger. Obviously they could count on him to look after Gabrielle when they were gone, but their daughter had become so fragile and he, Paul, so bitter, they feared that her health would worsen under such circumstances. What they wanted most for her was that she be able to regain control of herself and acquire a little independence. She was resistant, lacked confidence. For instance, Gabrielle's father told Jeanne that he kept renewing her driver's licence and often urged her to use the car for short distances. But she didn't want to get behind the wheel, as if she were the one responsible for her accident and was punishing herself.

They asked Jeanne how she had met Gabrielle, assumed that they must have been close friends because their daughter was so delighted by her visit. Marianne burst in: "Don't let them down!" So Jeanne lied a little so as not to let them down: yes, they'd been very close as students, inseparable even at one time. And the parents smiled because, in the end, that's all we have in this life: the power of such ties. Because Jeanne has brought back the past. Because Gabrielle was in such a wonderful mood today, in spite of her pain. Because they suddenly did not feel so alone with their anxiety and their hope. When Jeanne left to go to bed, Gabrielle's mother told her: "It was so nice of you to come; stay as long as you want."

Marianne, lurking somewhere in Jeanne's head, replied at once: "As long as you want, Jeanne dear, as long as you want."

That remark keeps reverberating. And Jeanne, staring out the window at the sky crowded with stars you don't see in the city, has the impression that since her birth there has been a black X on the calendar. But at the same time, it strikes her as senseless. To change your life as if you were flipping a pancake, as if the past had just been swept away by these individuals she barely knows. But she knows most of all that she's just hanging on by one hand. The other has never stopped looking for something to hold on to.

It's well known that the night belongs not to the world of reason, but to the world of visions. She allows one to appear, a familiar image that hasn't come to her since Marianne took off. She opens her eyes even wider onto the night, because images have all the answers. The park with its soft light, its trees, its bushes, its soothing smells. But empty, without a crowd. Only five individuals whom Jeanne, floating above them, can recognize. First of all, Gabrielle, arms held out to her, her parents a little farther away under the trees, reserved but just as insistent. Then, with his back to Gabrielle, Victor, his hands on his hips, flour-covered apron, squinting in the sun. Paul, very close to his sister, with his silence that's more powerful than a cry.

And each of them calls to her for himself, just for himself.

☾

Victor is calculating. The Germain family buys bread twice a week. Logically then, the day after tomorrow. Let's hope it isn't Gabrielle who comes, but her.

Dawn. His day has already begun. Like all the others. Actions repeated day after day, for such a long time now. The ingredients, the aroma of the yeast, the flour to be dampened, the steady sound of the dough mixer, the heat of the ovens, the triumphant colour of the loaves in the dark bakery. But above all, those blessed hours before he opens, before the first customer reminds him that the world is not made of bread alone, but also of distant looks and clattering coins, flung on the counter like swill to pigs.

Victor retains few memories of his life before the bakery. Not even his mother's face: erased. But now and then there are flashes: he's hungry, he's dirty and alone in a decaying room, his mother won't come home tonight, or she does come back and shuts herself away in the bedroom with a man, then another one, and another, till morning. He himself, huddled under a blanket on the battered sofa.

"Shut up and keep still!"

His mother's voice, a few words he remembers. Then one morning she doesn't come home, she won't come home ever again. A policeman arrives, a woman assumes responsibility for him, he's taken to the doctor, the dentist, someone buys clothes for him. Every time, he hears someone whisper: "Poor child!"

A week later, they explain that his grandparents are going to give him a home, pamper him. They don't come to get him. A trucker agrees to drive him, as long as he keeps quiet. Victor travels hundreds of kilometres sitting next to the driver, with all his possessions in a brown shopping bag at his feet. He sees nothing of the landscape, the windows of the truck are too high and he's too small.

Afterwards, though, everything becomes clear, perfectly imprinted on his memory. The driver helps him get down and opens the door of the bakery. The tinkling of the little bells. They go inside. No one. The truck driver tells him to wait. Goes away again. Victor doesn't dare set his bag on the floor. The aroma of the warm bread lined up on the shelves, the golden round loaves. Immediate enchantment. To Victor, bread will always represent his first and his only feeling of safety. The sound of footsteps coming from the back. His grandmother first, a net over her grey hair, a flowered apron, lavender. Then his grandfather. A tall man dressed in white, with a white cotton beret rammed onto his head. Unsmiling.

Finally his grandmother says: "Come here!"

They will not love this child, but won't hate him either. He won't be mistreated. These people have a strong sense of duty. They will bring him up in the religion of bread. They won't talk to him about his mother, who at sixteen ran away with a travelling salesman, ungrateful little hellcat from whom they heard nothing until the day when some stranger called to say that she'd been found lifeless near the pillars of a bridge and that they had been appointed to look after the child.

"The child? What child?" the grandmother had murmured.

"Your grandson, that's what child!" the voice on the phone hastened to reply.

The grandfather had been transfixed. A grandson, scrawny and shy, who at the age of seven had not yet started school.

The whole story had spread through the village. The couple had to confirm it. Victor was in any case the living proof. They'd brought home their daughter's remains without attracting attention, the priest had agreed to say a few prayers, since then she had been resting in the family plot.

Victor went to school. He was left out by the other children. Sometimes after class he would go to the cemetery. He learned to read and did his best to make out the inscription on his mother's tombstone. Her first name, but above all her family name, the same as his, the same as the name of the bakery. He hurried home. At this time of day, his grandfather would be cleaning and sweeping up. Victor knew instinctively that he wouldn't win his grandparents' love, but he also knew that he'd create a place for himself in this bakery that bore his name. His grandfather had actually understood that. And if Victor represented his daughter's sin, her shame and her humiliation, he also represented the future. As Victor's mother had been his only child, the boy and his fascination with bread, represented the only possible future for his bakery. And so he had undertaken to teach the boy the trade. The child had talent. He and his wife could grow old in peace. The boy would pay back his debt. Eventually, they retired. Victor, unwavering, looked after them. They had passed away within three months of one another and had joined their daughter in the shade of the big elm tree in the graveyard. Victor had inherited the bakery and a sum of money that allowed him to go on plying his trade in a village whose population was declining. And in spite of the competition from the sliced bread on grocery store shelves. The bakery was his spoils, his property, a gift that had not been intended for him but had ended up in his hands, to make amends for his childhood. Since the death of his grandparents, he'd lived on his own. He fled the village late on Saturday and came back the following day. He'd been seen hanging out in town on summer nights. Victor liked young men. After bread, they were his only passion. He had constructed his life discreetly around those two reference points. Asked for nothing more. Victor had a dream that he didn't consider to be attainable: to meet someone one day with whom he would feel at ease to be alive.

☾

When Jeanne called the restaurant at the last minute to tell them she wouldn't come to work the next day, her boss was angry and threatened to replace her for good. Shrugging, she hung up. Subject closed.

Gabrielle has been resting. For some days now her colour has come back. Today, Sunday, the village is asleep in the sunlight. The aroma of evergreens, their call. The mildness of the air, the warm light on her body. Jeanne feels like exploring. It's a good opportunity. She'll suggest to Gabrielle that they go for a drive: how can she persuade Gabrielle to drive again? "No," retorts Marianne, "not persuade, much simpler, just charm her."

"It's so sunny! We should go for a drive."

"Where?"

"I don't know. Around here; all I've seen since I got here is the village."

"It's the same everywhere else … the woods, the mountain."

Jeanne takes her hand.

"I know you're afraid, your parents told me. This isn't any kind of test, it's just for pleasure. We won't go far. I know: let's go and see your brother."

The suggestion has just popped into her mind, without premeditation. But with the impression that there is no other place in the world to be on this Sunday afternoon. Gabrielle hesitates, then agrees. The idea is reassuring. Jeanne beside her in the car, with Paul as their destination.

Gabrielle sits up straight, stiff, hands clenching the wheel. She doesn't meet another car. Gradually, she relaxes.

"See? Driving isn't something you forget, it's like skating!"

Jeanne has rolled down the window. She doesn't notice — not yet — the St. Pierre hill and its dangerous curve and then, further along, the enormous tamarack lost in the middle of the spruce trees. She doesn't mark her territory either. She is walking on new earth, totally carefree. She is discovering the new world as naively as someone who thinks he's reached the Indies.

There are hardly any houses on this forest road that's

taking them to Paul's, just a few grouped together where the road branches off to pass between two mountains.

"Why did he come to such an out-of-the-way place?" asks Jeanne.

Gabrielle replies that more than she does, Paul has this part of the country in his blood. A country with no future for its young people. All of whom have left it anyway. But he had bet that he'd be able to live here no matter what.

"No matter what," Gabrielle repeats insistently.

At sixteen he had left to continue his education outside. Since childhood he's wanted to become a veterinarian. He held firm, but he missed his own environment. Not the people, but the woods — the only space where he didn't feel cramped inside his skin. When he returned he seized an opportunity, bought the house and the land from a cousin of his father; that's where he would settle. And since the region had more forests than farms, he only worked part-time as a veterinarian. Which allowed him to work his wood lots. Paul had what he wanted: his childhood dream and the forest. He met a woman when he finished his studies, he brought her here but she didn't last a year. The isolation got to her. At the end of winter she gave him an ultimatum: either they move closer to civilization or she would leave. Paul didn't give in. She took off. He became more closed-in. Now and then he showed up with a girl from who knows where, he went through periods of intense rage, always directed at himself, which he knocked out with cases of beer. He would have become a monster had it not been for his charisma, the kind of unfettered beauty that emanated from him. He was highly thought of in the village: he'd chosen to make his life here.

Gabrielle toots the horn as soon as Paul's house appears. He's waiting for them, leaning against the handrail. She parks close to him. He doesn't move. It's the first time Jeanne has seen him smile. He takes them to the shore of the river that runs through his property.

All three are seated on stones warmed by the sun. Jeanne is trying to take in everything so she can bring it out again later, in case of emergency: the sound of the water, the birds in the foliage, the first insects of the season, the schools of tiny, famished trout in the cold, deep part of the river, and the light, yes, above all the light, which melts the distance between beings. Jeanne watches Gabrielle, the light that envelops her is healing; in a while she'll get up, her bones will be new, sturdy. A miracle, like at Fatima or Lourdes. And for Paul as well, perfectly relaxed at her side, the miracle takes effect. He who lacks words, who will always lack them, is naming, explaining with a multitude of details, to initiate Jeanne: the work in the woods, the exploitation of the forests.

The girls start for home at the end of the afternoon. Their faces are on fire, the first sunburn of the season. Paul follows them. They'll eat together as they do every Sunday.

—

But tonight will be a little like a party. For Gabrielle and her burst of enthusiasm today. At supper, they'll laugh. The parents will be as happy and innocent as children.

After dessert, when they're still at the table, Gabrielle suddenly begins to shiver. A powerful headache takes hold of her and sounds the end of the respite. She cries, claims she should have expected that she'd have to pay for her afternoon. The party's over.

Jeanne walks Paul to his van. They must accept something obvious: they are irretrievably united against Gabrielle's misfortune.

"If he were here in front of me, that guy who hit her, I'd kill him."

By speaking those words, it's the afternoon that Paul has just killed.

In the kitchen, the parents are waiting for Jeanne; before she goes upstairs to join their daughter, they beg her to stay for the summer.

4

It's so dark, the only thing Jeanne can see is a black mass in the middle of the clearing. For hours now she's been sitting on the stairs. Death takes a long time, you drag it around with you like a secret, like a stone chained to your ankle. It defies all beliefs. You could imagine it being deployed with searing intensity, taking as long as a lightning flash or a shot. Most of the time it takes another route. Discreetly, it accompanies you, walks along beside you and every so often, tortures. It chooses the body and its pain, that's its most visible route. Other times, it chooses the most deeply hidden fault, sneaks into it and stirs up everything along its way: that is its most perverse form. It rises up, opens old wounds: an austere childhood and its loneliness, a decisive country road one night in July, an injury, a rage that nothing can alleviate, love and the fear of abandonment, Siamese twins that share one heart.

Jeanne resigns herself to go inside. Generally, at this hour, when her son Jérôme is sleeping in the village, she phones to wish him good night. Has he finished his homework? Yes, Gabrielle has checked. What's he doing right now? Playing a video game with Gabrielle, but she's not an ideal partner, her hand isn't fast enough on the button. She hears Gabrielle protest. The child doesn't bid her good night, doesn't ask about her day, has just one question, always the same one in these circumstances. He wants to know if his father has come back.

"No," replies Jeanne in a neutral tone, with no explanation. Tonight she will not call her son.

She avoids turning too many lights on inside. For fear of scaring the moose. She has heated up some leftovers that she doesn't eat, as though it is imperative that she perform her usual tasks. She goes upstairs for a blanket. She wants to be back outside. From her bedroom window, the animal's shadow merges with the black bulk of the trees all around. Nothing is wasted, nothing is created: the order of the world and its biggest lie.

She stations herself on the veranda where the windows are open. The animal has just given out some little grunts and though she can make it out only vaguely, she senses a movement of its head.

Jeanne has brought out a bottle of cognac, she who drinks so little. Even lights a cigarette, she who hasn't smoked for years. A voice shouts: "You're being such an idiot!" She wishes she were hearing Marianne's voice, so infrequent now. But no, it's her own. "That's right, Jeanne, you're being such an idiot. For hours now you've been thinking you're indispensable to that moose, thinking he's chosen you, you in particular, because he's ended up outside your house; and admit it, you think he's chosen you so he won't die alone. If you go on searching, you'll have to face up to the fact that proximity never eradicates distance. That all you've been looking for since you've come here to live is to keep in motion those individuals who haven't found rest in your arms, and if you've sometimes had the impression that you were penetrating to their very souls, you know perfectly well it was just an illusion, a strategy to keep you from leaving them. You've crossed their threshold, that's all."

FOURTH STRAY BULLET

*I*n the village, people are talking. Who is that young woman behind the counter at the bakery? Victor's employee and paying guest at the Germains'? Very strange. As people have always steered clear of Victor, he's not the one they ask. Nor do they dare ask the young stranger, who doesn't appear inclined to chat, though she seems pleasant enough. In the end, they asked Gabrielle's parents, who replied simply that she was spending the summer with them, that she was a school friend of their daughter's. To the villagers, the explanation is satisfactory, but incomplete. Why did Victor hire her? He got along perfectly well on his own. In the country, everything must find its niche. Necessarily, one that's appropriate and clean. It's the only aspect that irritates Jeanne. She feels constantly spied on — not nastily, but she feels people's eyes on her all the same. They smile at her, say hello, but they're quick to examine her from top to bottom.

Jeanne hoped that Victor would introduce her to bread-making right away. He told her: "Later. Sales first." At first she was alone at the front of the bakery, serving customers who mainly came in the morning. There's no line-up at Victor's bakery, people buy enough bread for several days, and the village isn't densely populated. Jeanne spends long slack periods waiting for customers. At such times she thinks that she's totally ridiculous. Here she is, a young translator about to start working in her profession, standing with folded arms in a country bakery. But then it's better than drifting on her own above an anonymous crowd, better than letting herself be clutched by voices, faces, hands that will perhaps become warm arms wrapped around her. She strokes the blue glass beads around her neck.

Weary of twiddling her thumbs while she waits for customers, Jeanne has ended up with Victor in the back. She learns with her eyes. Is dying to get her hands in the bread dough. Don't rush things. Victor is a strange one. Sometimes he concentrates so hard, is so lost in thought, nothing can bring him back. The next moment, Jeanne becomes his exclusive centre of interest. It doesn't take her long to bring him out of his shell. A good pupil, she hasn't forgotten the Marianne Method: walk in without knocking, aim for the heart, look squarely in the eyes. Victor doesn't stand in her way. It's exactly what he's been expecting.

Jeanne and love. Like sleep, which every night deserts her. Eyes open in the darkness, quietly waiting. Fatigue next morning, but she's used to it. Makes do with four or five hours when she really needs eight. She lives through her days as if nothing were wrong.

Paul is prowling. Awkwardly. They've all noticed. Gabrielle and her parents hold their breath: this could become permanent. But Jeanne pretends to see nothing, feigns indifference, and keeps busy responding to those who send her tangible signals, who hold out their hands quite openly, who speak to her with words. And Paul, walled up inside his rage and his desire, hasn't yet figured out how.

One morning at the bakery, Victor asks quite straightforwardly if there's something going on between her and Paul. Jeanne, surprised by his sudden familiarity, denies it.

He explains to her that he would just as soon steer clear of Paul. Because of the mute contempt that certain men have for men who aren't like them. The difference between them like a threat, an assault. Paul didn't come for bread before Jeanne set foot inside the bakery. Gabrielle or her mother took care of it. Now he comes often. Sometimes just to drive her home at the end of the day. Never does Paul say a word to him. Jeanne tries without conviction to persuade Victor that he mustn't attach importance to such details; Paul is unsociable, he approaches everyone from on high.

"See, you're taking his side!" he replies ironically.

He lays it on to annoy her, but it doesn't happen. She's happy. Victor has scored a point, has opened his arms a little wider. It's beginning to resemble the notion of intimacy she has formed. One day, she thinks, there'll be no more space between them, he'll experience her fear of being no one and she, the anxiety that he hides, that gnaws away at him and overpowers him. In a word, it's a question of trust between sherpas.

Victor has asked Jeanne to stay after closing. A straight staircase at the very back of the bakery. He lives up there, where he once lived with his grandparents. The place where he dreams, sleeps, eats. The lair of the other Victor, the one who takes on his own odour as he sheds that of the bread. Unlike the main floor, the upstairs is bathed in light. Jeanne is fascinated. She wouldn't have imagined him living in a place like this. In fact he is still living with his grandparents. Has altered nothing. Everything is intact: the old-fashioned and modest furniture, the objects, rugs, curtains. An outdated and overcrowded atmosphere, as if those who had lived here before him had crammed their lives into that space without discarding anything. Victor kept up the house with the respect that is owed to sanctuaries. That too is part of the gift his grandparents bequeathed him, by default. Here and there, signs of the present: an open bottle of gin on the low table in the living room, the ashtray full of butts, a cat dozing in the sun at a window, and in the kitchen, dirty dishes on the counter.

Victor plays tour guide. With detailed explanations and silent pauses. Each room has its history, its historic family event, its small abrasion. The last door he opens is the one to his childhood bedroom. They sit on the bed, side by side. The yellowed blind is pulled down. Along the way, he grabbed the bottle of gin in the living room, two glasses in the kitchen. Jeanne accompanies him, though she hates gin more than any other drink. Not for anything would she break this moment. Victor is talking. He's about to become a child again, to unveil that child to her. Without emotion, without trying for Jeanne's pity, as if here were speaking about some other child, from a book or a movie.

He doesn't linger. It wasn't to tell about his childhood that he brought Jeanne up here. He points to the massive armoire, along with the bed the only piece of furniture in the room. Inside, carefully stacked on the shelves, are several hundred copies of *National Geographic*. The buried treasure. Victor's collection. Every issue, not one missing, he declares, for the past twenty-five years. Jeanne bursts out laughing. Victor is slightly offended.

"No, don't get mad. I'm surprised, that's all. You, who've never left the village! I don't see you as an explorer."

All the issues have been classified. Victor has used coloured cards to separate them and indicate the year they were published. A few copies, he keeps in an envelope. They're old, very rare, faded.

"Jeanne, there's something I'd like to ask you ..."

Without hesitating he takes two issues from the shelf and shows her two lavishly illustrated articles. One on the Amazonian forest, the other about the desert of the Sahara.

"Can you translate them for me?"

Victor's images, his dreams without words, his illiterate's journeys. He has turned his childhood over to her for good.

"You want them written out?"

"No, just read them tonight, tomorrow you can tell me everything."

"Why those two in particular?"

"They're my favourites. But I've got others too that I'd like you to translate."

Jeanne glances at her watch.

"Okay, I'd better be going. Gabrielle will be worried."

Six o'clock. Jeanne is walking down the main street with the *National Geographics* under her arm. At this time of day the whole village is sitting at their tables over their soup. Through open windows she can hear scraps of voices and kitchen sounds. There's one house at the end of the street where she is expected. They won't start eating without her. A young woman has been waiting all day for her. She'll be

proud to take her into the garden, which is practically explod-
ing in the heat. After supper, they'll water it till nightfall.

Stretched out on the living room sofa, holding an empty
gin bottle, the baker is waiting for the evening and the night
to pass. Waiting for the bread. Waiting for Jeanne to come
back with the images from his dreams multiplied by words.

On a forest road, a man hesitates. To the right, his parents'
house, to the left, his own. He is waiting for a young woman
who has come from somewhere else to recognize him, to
take him with his anger and his silence. Without negotiating.

Jeanne, slightly breathless, quickens her pace. A car speeds
up, two dogs dash across the street. If you are expected, you
can't be abandoned. Happiness, for a fraction of a second.

☾

Summer, its fire, the strident song of insects, flowers on
balconies, the sleeping mountain. Time, its music slow as love.

The days with Victor. Evenings reassuring Gabrielle. The
sleepless nights at the four corners of the planet, nose in the
National Geographic. And the images over which she's lost
control. Jeanne no longer floats above the familiar park, but
above a forest, a river. A man who reminds her of Marianne,
up to his knees in water, in the middle of the river, holds
down a canoe with his arm. Week after week he thinks up

ways to spend his Sundays. His fear of being washed away, drowned. His fondness for the water.

((

Jeanne has to acknowledge it: she can't do anything for Gabrielle. When she saw her again she sensed a kind of appeal. Thought she could help her. Believed it. Believed she would give her back her drive, her appetite for life. Neither Paul's insistent defeatism when he tries to reason with her, her own illusions about his sister, nor Victor's silence when she talks to him at great length about Gabrielle has shaken her fervour. Not at first, anyway. But summer is advancing and despite the parents' naive tenacity, Jeanne is well aware that it's not just a question of bones and muscles. Nor of phobias or anxiety. Gabrielle's pain sails in deeper waters. Devastated zones. Irreparable. To her great surprise, Jeanne isn't all that far from Paul, with his rage and his lust for revenge.

At times, Gabrielle sinks into a universe where everything proves her wrong. She locks herself away inside herself, doesn't eat, sleeps a lot, cries for hours. The slightest detail becomes a tragedy: some worm-eaten cabbages in the garden, a cake left too long in the oven. The opportunity to treat herself as less than nothing. It can go on for days. At other times she regresses, takes refuge in a childlike attitude. Sulks or gets overexcited about nothing. Manipulates and waits for others to decide for her. But also, between these periods of crisis, the luminous, fragile Gabrielle, defenceless, victim of a bastard who decided one night that there wouldn't be a guilty party. Gabrielle, her small courage held tight against her chest, with her enormous heart, her mocking laugh, and her instinctive gift for affection. Almost the Gabrielle from before.

Jeanne thinks that summer won't last forever, that one day she will have to leave. She says so often, to convince herself. When she's with Victor, surrounded by loaves of bread and rolls, telling him about the probable extinction of the Royal Bengali tigers, a faithful translation of the latest issue he's given her. With Gabrielle, during their tedious weeding sessions. With Paul on Sundays, when Gabrielle pleads a headache to leave them alone, the black water of Otter Lake, the gliding of oars the only words.

☾

A fair in the village. A tent has been put up, with games for the children and the old people. The others drink beer, eat corn on the cob. Paul and Jeanne try to persuade Gabrielle — who's going through a rough period — to come and check it out.

"Too noisy, too much shouting, too many people!" she protests.

"But we'll be there with you, for you."

Gabrielle replies with a forced smile and stops resisting.

"Okay, okay, but not this afternoon, just for the show tonight."

They've won. A victory over Gabrielle's darkness.

Paul gets an emergency call from a farmer. He won't be spending Sunday with the girls. He'll come back for them early that evening. From the gallery Jeanne, disappointed, watches him go to his van. His thighs, his worn jeans, the air that he displaces. Paul, who never says goodbye when he leaves people, turns around towards her. An expression that she hasn't seen before, strained and ironic: he's picked up on Jeanne's disappointment.

Gabrielle takes a nap to conserve her strength, her parents are already at the party; for Jeanne, stretched out on a chaise longue, this afternoon is endless.

Paul is back shortly after six. Showered, shaved, changed. But in a foul mood. Gabrielle is hesitant again, isn't sure she feels like going out. Betrayal, thinks Jeanne, looking daggers at Paul.

In the van, Paul doesn't speak, Gabrielle is wearing her hangdog look. Jeanne fulminates. Paul's moods. The world stops turning, the song is becoming familiar. At the bakery, she asks him to stop.

—

"Go on ahead, I'll catch you later. I have to see Victor."
She gets out without saying anything more. Gabrielle, disconcerted, tries to hold back her tears; Paul steps on the gas.

Jeanne goes to the back of the bakery, then up the outside staircase to where Victor lives. The grass hasn't been cut, it's full of weeds, he says he maintains a wild garden. She hears the TV through the screen door. She knocks, he doesn't answer. Decides to go in just as he appears in the kitchen.

"Victor!"

His upper lip is split and swollen, above his eye too. A bottle of gin in one hand, an ice-pack in the other.

"What are you doing here?" he shouts, irritated.

"I had a hunch," she lies. "Did you have an accident?"

"If you really want to know, sweetheart, I'll tell you."
He's come up to her, planted himself in front of her, his face so close, he reeks of alcohol.

"Last night I went into town, I killed time for part of the night. I met somebody. I got beat up, he got my wallet. You want more details? You want to hear about the other times? Because needless to say this wasn't the first. Is that what you came for?"

He stops talking, out of breath, calms down. Jeanne says nothing. They stand there face to face, not moving. Then Victor rests his forehead against Jeanne's.

"Go away, please, but don't be late tomorrow morning, I don't want customers to see me like this."

—

95

She kisses him on the mouth and leaves.

The show inside the tent got underway a few minutes ago. The place is packed. People laugh and talk while on the makeshift stage, a young local talent croaks out a current hit at the top of his lungs.

It takes Jeanne a few minutes to spot Gabrielle, who is sitting at the front with her parents and her cousins. She looks as if she's having fun. She beckons to Jeanne to join them. It's Paul whom Jeanne is looking for. She suspects that he's left. Checks out the place several times, finally spots him at the back. Sitting at a picnic table, with two empty beer bottles in front of him and holding a third. He's feigning interest in the show. He has seen Jeanne looking for him.

She sits down beside him, very close. No reaction. There won't be words between them. Jeanne is waiting for a gesture, so is Paul. The entire future, everything they will be together is contained in the precise moment when one of them breaks the silence. They're nearly touching. He downs his beer, gulping nervously. Jeanne sits erect, motionless, tense, arms at her sides, hands on her thighs. On the stage they've switched to country: your cheatin' heart … It could be simple. She would rest her head on his shoulder. He'd put his arm around her. That would be the start. No need to make other efforts, only glide along the water in the sunlight, like that Sunday in the canoe. In front of Jeanne, the crowd, the singer. But above all, there, under her eyelids when she closes her eyes for a second, the back of Paul's neck, his mouth, his body: inaccessible, yet about to be offered. But it's not that simple. It's like a war, she thinks, just before the hostilities; no, not a war, that's too harsh. It's like a brief pause along a narrow path on the edge of a deep crevice. The only possible road. Oxygen is scarce, the pack heavy on one's back. Fear, loneliness. The promise. The crazy dream. They are glued to the bench. Each one knows he won't get up before the other.

And because things end up happening, because on the stage, love songs with their empty words follow one another inevitably, because time flies — this evening, youth, life — Paul grabs Jeanne's arm. Squeezes it tight. Both of them still looking straight ahead. She could interpret his move as a conquest, a commitment. But that's not what Paul's fingers pressing on her skin are telling her. He has grabbed her arm as if the edge of the path had just crumbled while they were walking, as if they've both nearly fallen into the void. And now they are measuring their luck and the danger on the road they'll have to take.

His hand doesn't loosen its grip. In Jeanne's head a collision of images: the park, the hole in the earth; Marianne's arms; Victor's jungles and deserts; the kitchen in the Italian restaurant; the years of good behaviour; the articles to translate; Gabrielle left for dead in the ditch; Paul's house, remote, tucked away between two mountains; the pitch-black nights in this part of the world; the delirium of the stars.

Jeanne will respond. With a movement. Doesn't know what form it will take. It will be a movement that must have the force of the words she won't utter, that are seething with impatience in her throat. Words that say all right, this evening, this night, tomorrow, what's left of the summer, of life also, she consents — no, she takes the risk. But he has to know that she isn't just staying for him. She is staying for Gabrielle, at the base camp, to keep the fire burning and show him that she's part of the expedition. She is staying for Victor, because of the altitude, the fatigue, and the sherpas' mutual respect. Yes, she is staying for him, Paul, for the pressure of his hand, insistent, intensified, on her arm, for his silence and his appeals, for the bodies' promise. But he must know as well as she does that it's an unusual expedition that is setting off, an expedition with no sherpas. Only two strange explorers, together but separate, lucid but unconscious. Yes, truly an unusual expedition. A demanding ascent. A pointless conquest.

A movement, just a movement. The back of her hand on Paul's thigh, her fingers slowly opening. The caress, the first.

He gets up: "We're going." No anger or tension in his voice. Only his usual stiffness. They're leaving the fair. On stage, more hearts, still cheatin'.

They cross the deserted village. Paul drives slowly. As if it has to last, this moment before, this moment when they don't know anything, this moment when they still are part of mythology, where they have not become an ordinary couple in a messy bedroom at dawn.

At the bakery, Jeanne casts a worried look. Yes, she'll come in earlier tomorrow morning, that's a promise. At the limit of the village, the family house and its bedroom, empty tonight, not a desertion, no, Gabrielle, an absence that is taking root.

The forest road, the huge silence, the total darkness. Paul is driving faster. Ahead of them, in the middle of the road, appears what Jeanne thinks is a big grey dog. Running, running, right into the headlights. Paul matches the speed of the van to the animal's. Laughs.

"Slow down, you're harassing him."

He slows, letting the animal disappear into the night.

"Why didn't he go to the side of the road?" Jeanne wonders.

"Because he doesn't know that danger, he doesn't know how to run away from it."

"Doesn't know how to run away, doesn't know how to run away," she repeats to herself. And on this night that is now beginning, that is the beginning of a story, she hopes that it's not an omen.

5

It's getting late. The moose is still alive. Jeanne is incapable of leaving the veranda. She wouldn't be able to sleep in any case. On the nights that she spends alone in the house, when Paul disappears and their son, Jérôme, stays over in the village, she refuses to give in to sleep and then, in the middle of the day, she's out like a light. She claims that it's a way to hold the fort.

"What is there to protect?" asks Victor, annoyed, when he sees that she's helpless, tired.

He maintains that she chooses not to sleep on those nights, to punish herself.

"Punish myself for what?" she asks in turn.

This night, at least, there really is something to protect, and for once she's paying attention to something other than her own problems. If Jeanne can no longer distinguish anything outside, inside the light is pushing its way in, encouraged by the bottle of cognac and the pack of cigarettes she's in the process of emptying. She can't venture any further into excess, can Jeanne-the-moderate, who had aspired to a simple life, with open arms, arms that would recognize her, that would name her every time they opened — and they would open frequently, constantly.

She has arranged the cushions from the garden chairs on the veranda table. She sits there now, her back against a window. The ideal position from which to dominate the situation. She has turned up the thermostat, left the kitchen door open. It's comfortable despite the temperature, which has dropped as darkness fell. The night can be long, she has everything she needs: images, words — those that come so easily when one's alone — the lightness that alcohol brings, the weight of the smoke in the lungs. And anguish.

Too bad it's a moonless night. The only hitch: not to be able to make out the dark mass in the clearing.

The voice of Marianne: "You, Jeanne, you're going to choose an uncomplicated life." As if she'd been cut from a modest fabric, neutral in colour, woven tightly to last. She remembers, that remark had offended her. She'd concluded that Marianne had said it to emphasize her lack of every-thing: of cleverness, of charm, of personality. Six thousand, eight hundred and nine days after that truth, decreed by a girl who thought she was the centre of the universe, and was. "Life is so complicated!" murmurs Jeanne as she closes her eyes to taste the passage, the burn of the alcohol and the tobacco deep in her throat.

FIFTH STRAY BULLET

*S*eptember has arrived on the sly. The nights are gradually getting cooler. Gabrielle and her father have put together some plastic shelters to protect the plants from the cold at night, to extend the life of the garden. In a few days the light has changed. The shape and texture of the clouds as well. The mountain is announcing its colours timidly, another few weeks and the grand final exuberance will come as a reminder of the silence and the reserve that will follow during the winter months.

Jeanne hasn't left. She takes the best without further ado. She is the queen, the momentary heroine of a small group of people who ask only to smile. What power, what incredible force, she thinks, to believe that she holds all the strings as she pleases, to think that people are happy simply because she is there, solicitous, holding their heads in her hands.

She has moved in with Paul, into the white house tucked in between the mountains. "Home," she thinks, looking around her: the forest, the clearing, the narrow, winding dirt road. "My home? My home, really?" Surprised, an outsider, she would like to touch the wood of every tree in these forests to make it be true, to make it last, to make Paul's anger, neutralized by her presence in his bed every night, not come back, so the part of him that is not violent would triumph over the other. Perhaps, there, yes, it is her home.

Victor is torn between contradictory feelings. She isn't leaving, that's the main thing. That girl who, every day for more than three months now, makes him tell everything, has given him back the words, the simplest and the crudest, has gathered them in her hands like bread dough. The girl he waits for every morning, before the customers come, the girl who's come from somewhere else, a stranger to everything he loathes about this village: the prejudices, the silent contempt, the dogged curiosity, the ignorance. The girl who is so polite — too polite, almost — her self-possessed manner, her reserve, her discreet fervour, but also her plea, like his own, her plea for a place to accommodate love. Because it is love. Victor does love that girl, like a partner, a sister, like the young woman who took the place of his mother in another life, who sleeps now with all her misery behind the church, between her parents. He loves that girl like a family rediscovered late in life, after years of wandering in refugee camps. The problem, though, is that she doesn't come alone. She comes with the clan she has chosen, who have chosen her. Who embody everything he would like to erase from the surface of the earth: a close-knit family, helpless parents, a man who has spent less time with her than he has and who has taken away her fear of being no one. And then, the unbearable. Gabrielle. The very image of disaster. The tap of her cane on the bakery's tile floor. Who seems to say when she pays for her bread: "No hope, Victor, no hope for the wounded. No healing. I will stay locked away inside my parents' house like you in your bakery. On the fringe, always on the fringe of life." Her sad, angelic smile, her broken gait when he holds the door open for her. Victor's relief when he shuts it again.

Gabrielle can breathe now. Jeanne has stayed. She won't leave. Doesn't stop promising. Everywhere, the signs: in her hand that strokes her brother's shoulders, in the heavy baskets that she carries for her from garden to house, in the contented look on her face at the aroma of fruit cooked with sugar. But most of all Jeanne has stopped insisting. She no longer tries to push her into places where she doesn't want to go. No longer exhorts her to become again the Gabrielle she was before. That one has vanished, Jeanne has finally stopped looking for her. She is the first person to look at her with that expression. Gabrielle, infinitely grateful, tells herself that her future is contained precisely in that gaze.

☾

Jeanne is trying to put her new life in order. Above all, not depend on others. Which is to say, Paul and Victor. With the latter, things have been quickly clarified. He doesn't really need her at the bakery. Oh, sure, she spared him the chore of dealing with customers during the summer, but it's expensive, having an employee, even at a crummy salary as Victor says, half-amused, half-embarrassed, when he slips the meagre wad of bills into her apron pocket every Thursday.

"Victor, I don't want to be a lady-in-waiting disguised as a baker's helper. I don't want to be paid for that. The woman who's enjoying herself here, who's in the process of reading every article published in *National Geographic* over the past twenty-five years — she won't disappear. But the woman who every day serves customers, takes bread from the oven, spreads icing on sweet rolls, the woman you pay to do a job you've always been able to do on your own — for her, the summer-long adventure was convenient, pleasant, but in the long term it couldn't be justified. It would end up as a kind of charity."

"Is it Paul who doesn't want you coming here any more?" Victor asks curtly.

Every fit of anger in Jeanne's life — past and still to come — can be counted on the fingers of one hand. Victor is witnessing, stunned, the erupting volcano that is her reply. They end up laughing about it in each other's arms. But he, sly fox, won't have lost everything: she'll come once a week, on Thursday, the day when the whole village has passed the word that today is the day to buy bread.

Jeanne went back to the city for a while in the hope of finding translation work. She knocked on every door, got down on her knees. Played her cards with the energy of a convict. A miracle. Finally she gets one. A big book. Practical. A subject that doesn't interest her. A scandalous fee. Her honour safe. Paul won't consider that she owes him everything. He's come to the city to pick her up. Jeanne is waiting for him on the sidewalk, sitting on her cartons: her books — Italian cookbooks, dictionaries, grammars, novels, and collections of poems that she dreams of translating — her winter clothes, her memories. And most of all, leaning against the brick wall, her precious bicycle that has ended its first career and that one day her son will use, grudgingly, "an antique," he'll complain.

The veranda, Jeanne's favourite part of the house. It had been both vestibule and storeroom before she moved in. She has appropriated it for herself. Disposed of the objects and products for veterinary or forest use that were piled in every which way. She has set herself up there to work. When she's forced out by the cold she'll move to one of the empty bedrooms upstairs and make it her winter quarters.

There was just one detail to sort out. Jeanne wanted to be able to visit Gabrielle whenever she wished. And Victor. She intended to use her meagre savings to buy a very old car. Paul was strongly opposed: "A coffin on wheels!" One night Jeanne found a used car in good condition in front of the house. She wanted to pay him. He refused.

"It's a present," he told her.

They confronted one another. She forced him to accept her savings. Paul has understood something he already knows: every explorer wants to be the first and only one to plant the flag.

☾

Day by day, Jeanne is coming to grips with her life and with the world that surrounds her from the veranda. Paul leaves early, comes home late. Days at a time with her dictionaries and grammar books, with hares and flights of ducks that dare to venture right up to the door of the house, attracted by the grass in the clearing. A solitude that fits her body perfectly.

It is a time of abundance. The date should be carved into the bark of trees and into memories. A time of balance and intelligence where there is something for each of them, in her own actions as well as in his. A time when every morning has unprecedented consequences. They aren't afraid of getting carried away when faced with the obvious, they're no longer surprised by their happiness or by the splendour of the landscape. They are there, alive, not even winded. They had imagined that such a thing wouldn't happen until they'd reached the summit; so far they've covered only half the distance. And they can't get over their astonishment. In spite of suspicion, its rough music deep inside their ears.

☾

If it's absolutely necessary to look for losers in this story, just now Victor and Gabrielle seem to qualify. On the one hand, Jeanne is there, they acknowledge, but on the other hand, she has left them. Gabrielle no longer sees her every day, no longer hears her in the bedroom next door. A little death on the days when Jeanne doesn't drop in. She tries to ignore that additional discomfort, but life is so still once again, her world so closed-in on itself, and her parents, with their solicitude, can only reaffirm the boundaries of the territory. Paul drops in as often as before, but these are flying visits. A woman is waiting for him in a house on the Saint-Janvier road. He has his life, Gabrielle tells herself, *he* has a life. But there are other days too, when Jeanne turns up with plans for the two of them, simple, reassuring plans, and now that Jeanne has a car, even jaunts into town.

Victor, too, reasons with himself. Like Gabrielle, Jeanne's everyday absence sends him back to a powerful solitude that he'd blacked out over the course of a summer. Sometimes he is surprised to find himself feeling jealous of Paul.

A remarkable sensation that he gets rid of as best he can, which is to say badly, with big slugs of gin. He laughs at it sometimes. If anyone had told him that one day … jealous, and over a woman! Seeing Jeanne only on Thursday has created a kind of urgency, a demand to talk with her, be with her, to satisfy her wishes. The day will come. For Victor, there's no doubt about it, one day or one night she'll come into the bakery in tears, with a split lip, a black eye — then they will be brother and sister absolutely — Paul's rage will have turned against her. She'll have brought a few things and will beg him to take her back to where she comes from. That's the way, he's certain, he will lose her. For Victor, love always ends with a fight.

Every Thursday, he sets out to complete her apprenticeship. Jeanne no longer arrives when the bakery opens, but before the sun is even up, when Victor starts his day. He'll show her everything, she has to know as much about bread as he does. She's delighted, it's what she has been hoping for since the beginning. He underestimated her: she has observed him so closely, for months, that she's learned a lot more than he thought. Jeanne thinks that now they will be absolutely brother and sister.

☾

Her first winter in this part of the country. Short days. The whiteness of the landscape. An isolation that would give her vertigo if it weren't for the beginning of this love, this love that is sufficient unto itself. It is her first winter of submission. To the climate first, which determines her comings and goings, the road being often impassable because of the force of the wind and the accumulation of snow. Next, to the texts that she translates patiently, religiously, that every morning send her into a room for that peculiar encounter of two languages forced to understand and answer to each other. And then to the love to which she gives herself without fury, but also without reservation.

Paul resembles this land in winter: opaque, silent, seductive. Jeanne can't get over his silence, can't get over living in such silence. For her, words are the key to the world. Her life with him is light years from her own world. She spends hours every day making sure of the meaning of words, watching for any possible nuances or ambiguities, with the thought constantly in her mind that at the other end of her work there is someone demanding, anticipating words that match the original message. Sitting across from Paul at the table in the evening, she watches him, tranquil, nearly smiling, as he withdraws into his silence. She waits for him to speak. Nothing comes. A kind of unhealthy anxiety grabs her by the throat, but she represses it at once, asks him how his day was. He always answers economically, a few remarks, a few words only. But Jeanne's questions never annoy him. He's a man who gets along without words, that's all. Most likely because he has long since understood that he doesn't need them; the fascination he exerts on anyone who approaches him speaks for itself. And he knows how to operate with what he is, he's perfectly aware of how his silence affects Jeanne. As he isn't stupid, because he's promised himself that things would work out with her, he knows what limits not to cross, what weapons to deploy as well. For words, there are others, fortunately. Especially Victor. Jeanne notes the difference. All the words that Paul refuses, Victor offers her, lays at her feet. And she repays him.

"Thursday's your big outing!" he jokes, referring to the streams of words that she deals out as soon as she steps inside the bakery at dawn.

Victor no longer asks Jeanne to translate articles. Because words are precious and more infrequent now that he only sees her on Thursday. They no longer meet in the arid Mongolian steppes or the swampy plains of the Everglades; they've settled into a wild and secret region that doesn't appear on any maps or in any issue of *National Geographic*. A land of bread and words where each of them gives the other something he didn't think he would ever reveal. Victor knows all about Paul's silences, his outbursts, his touching surrenders, about Gabrielle's crises and frights; Jeanne, about the men who slip silently into Victor's life for the duration of a Saturday night in town. Their Thursday homeland. Unique, irreplaceable, even if each of them lives there only one day a week.

((

A phone call in the middle of the night. The first few times, Jeanne rushes to answer, thinking of Gabrielle. But it's always for Paul, who gets up immediately, pulls on some clothes, and leaves, griping. She manages to snatch a few bits of information: a calving that's going badly, a calf that's presenting abnormally. She can't get back to sleep and that is how her nights of solitary vigil begin. Paul comes home at dawn, showers, gets back into bed with her, and picks up his night where he'd left it. She pretends to be asleep and when Paul's breathing tells her that he has sunk into sleep, she gets up.

When the phone rings at the end of a bitterly cold night, Jeanne, who hasn't had much sleep, doesn't stir. Paul answers: "Yes?" Then silence. He switches on the bedside light and holds out the receiver.

"It's for you."

Victor, whose bad flu has developed into pneumonia, announces the apocalypse, that is, he won't be able to bake, he wants her to come right away.

The scene is unfolding in reverse. It's she who is hurrying, dressing in haste, doing her best to explain the situation. From the bed, Paul, propped on one elbow, watches her bustling about. Jeanne won't notice anything right away, too pressed for time to linger, but she'll have to admit, it was that night when anger resumed its place on Paul's face, when the wound reopened.

In his bed, Victor seems smaller. He has trouble breathing, complains of twinges in his back. His body is feverish, his eyes empty. Jeanne goes through the medicine chest; there must be a thermometer in this house. "Oh no, 40.5, that's impossible!" she thinks, panicking, as she applies a cool compress to Victor's forehead.

"You have to go to the hospital, you'll have to gather your strength."

Strength he does not possess; he doesn't react, murmurs: "Yes, yes."

Jeanne takes charge of the operations.

"Let me do it."

From closet and drawers she selects clothes, surprised that they're put away so neatly. She hasn't seen them before, they're in dark, sober colours, have no wrinkles or long streaks of flour.

She has pulled up the covers. He's shivering. A child. She dresses him. Her movements slow. Victor's efforts despite the inertia of his muscles. His thin naked body, Jeanne's gentle hands that brush against, that touch his body. The absence of awkwardness. Their perfect understanding of the moment.

Then, suddenly, reality emerges, sweeping Jeanne into the truth of images: Paul, in the bedroom, lying on his back, unable to sleep; the bakery, closed today, a weekday, for the first time in fifty years; the road to travel tonight to the hospital, the snow, the fir trees, Victor asleep in the car; finally the city, and the day that is dawning as it comes into view. Jeanne wondering if she's gigantic or minute.

Double pneumonia, the X-rays show clearly. The doctor hesitates. Should he keep Victor under observation or send him home?

"Does he live alone?"

Jeanne answers before he can.

"No."

The doctor hands her a prescription and points out that it could take a long time: a month, maybe two. But at least the very high fever should drop significantly in the next forty-eight hours, with the antibiotics he's prescribed.

On the way home, Victor is restless.

"A month or two! That's impossible, the bakery can't be closed for so long, that's forever! People will buy their bread at the grocery store, they'll get used to it, they won't come back, it will be the end!"

"I'll look after the bakery; it won't be as good, but they'll understand."

Victor knows that she can almost do it, that in fact there's no other solution. Jeanne holds his fate in her hands. It will be simple, after all. He relaxes and doesn't say another word on the way home.

Now it is Jeanne who silently, hands clutching the wheel, is restless. The bakery, the translation to finish before winter is over, Paul, Gabrielle. Not so simple after all.

They come back in the middle of the afternoon. Victor says that by now the whole village must realize that the bakery hasn't opened. He adds: "Check out the streets, I'm sure there'll be a rumour or two making the rounds."

Victor, exhausted, has collapsed onto his bed, with all his clothes on, knocked out. Jeanne has gone downstairs to the bakery. Everything is in its proper place, neat and tidy, as if it were Sunday. In the window of the door she puts a note: "Open Tomorrow." No sooner has she done so than a car slows down to read it. Tomorrow the whole village will come to find out what's going on.

Jeanne goes back upstairs; Victor is asleep, his old cat standing guard at the foot of the bed. The daylight is fading; outside, the snow is turning blue. She falls asleep in the big living room armchair.

When she wakes with a start it's completely dark. It's six o'clock, she's hungry, Victor should eat something too. The fridge and pantry are practically empty. Not even any bread! Briefly, standing in the middle of the kitchen, Jeanne has the impression that she is in the body of an unknown woman. Paradoxically, she inhabits that body in a way that she has never inhabited her own. "In full possession of her faculties": that idiotic expression springs to her lips when she wants to apply words to what she's feeling. For the first time in her life — and this discovery, this particular circumstance, alone in this kitchen, will be imprinted on her memory more permanently than a brand — Jeanne exists for someone else absolutely, vitally. She exists amid desire and need. "I want you there": this is what Victor wants to tell her. So Everest doesn't have just one summit, just one road, she thinks, surprised; there are many and we can go there simultaneously, with different partners.

She phones Gabrielle, describes her day in detail, explains the situation at great length and, most important, mentions that there's nothing to eat at Victor's. Gabrielle — the Gabrielle whose plan had once been to save humanity — springs to life.

"I'll make something, don't worry."

Half an hour later, she appears in the bakery with enough to feed at least half a dozen. After Gabrielle has gone, Jeanne phones Paul. Repeats the story.

"I'm not coming home tonight, I'm sleeping here. Tomorrow, I'll be looking after the bakery and Victor."

He shows neither empathy nor annoyance. Repeats "Fine," after each of Jeanne's sentences.

"Please drop by the bakery tomorrow morning."

She stands there motionless, holding the receiver, after he hangs up. How long can a silence go on? At what distance does the silence between two beings become an abyss?

☾

A bakery is a wonderful domain. Especially at five a.m., when you're alone with the whirr of the dough mixer, with the warmth and the first aromas of baking bread. Jeanne feels like a fish in water. Mind you, the customers have to be content with two basic breads, no dinner rolls or sweet rolls. Only the essential services. She won't be able to bake as much bread as Victor would have done, for lack of experience. It's so strange, she thinks, this sense of freedom and power that comes with making bread. This lightness in her motions, at once precise and urgent. At ten o'clock, yes, there will be bread on the shelves for customers, *her* bread, her work, a little like the day when she'll see her name on a book as translator for the first time — if that day ever comes — even printed in Lilliputian letters beneath the title of a novel on an inside page, not even on the cover, unlike her Anglophone colleagues.

Jeanne is running. Breadmaking requires second-by-second vigilance, a brief inattention and the whole batch, while it won't be lost, will have a crust that's a little too dark, a little too crisp. Now and then she dashes upstairs, leaving a whitish trail behind her, like a comet. She forces Victor to finish his orange juice. Is there anything particular that he fancies?

"Yes. Peace and bread that's not burned to a crisp."

Victor, his humour that is like distress in every circumstance.

Ten o'clock. Jeanne wouldn't use the word "crowd," that would be an exaggeration, given the number of people who live in this village, but it's close. The customers who come make inquiries. They're interested in Victor. "Pneumonia, that's all." They look surprised, disappointed almost, so that's all. She would have liked to add: "No, it's not AIDS, there's been no wrongdoing or arrest." After all, the people here remember his mother.

Because of the first wave of customers, one batch of bread is ruined. How does Victor manage to be everywhere at once? The shelves empty faster than she'd expected. By noon they'll be out of bread. She won't be able to make more.

Just then Gabrielle shows up. To check that everything's all right.

"Can I give you a hand?"

She sees that Jeanne is beginning to be swamped. And she, having missed out on a career as redeemer, is quick to realize that there's a way for her to practise it here, today. Jeanne has stationed her behind the counter, then gone back to her kneading and her ovens. The day ends in jubilation. "All we can do is laugh," says Jeanne; "tomorrow will be better." Gabrielle has had a wonderful day, you can see it on her face, she observes that pneumonia can last a long time, as if to ensure that her pleasure will go on for a while.

Once Gabrielle has gone, Jeanne finishes cleaning and tidying. In the window she places the "Open Tomorrow" sign, but she hasn't bolted the door, Paul might still come by. Night has fallen, she has switched on all the lights in the bakery so he will know that she's there, because she's well aware that he wouldn't go up to Victor's apartment. No doubt she knows her way around butterflies. A few minutes later, attracted by the light, Paul bursts into the bakery.

He doesn't move. Jeanne goes to him. Tries to look him up and down. He says nothing, as usual, he strokes her hair to brush away the flour. She tells him a little about her day and about Victor. Once again, she won't come home this evening. He mustn't say the wrong thing, he who goes running in the middle of the night, in all kinds of weather, to see a cow in distress — surely Victor's just as important as a cow in distress. No, he simply draws her to him, a forthright gesture, nestles his head in her hair, breathes deeply; when he frees himself, he smiles and leaves. A shudder runs through Jeanne: he has just shown her his anger in its most pitiful form.

((

After a while, Jeanne and Gabrielle have reached their cruising speed. The customers, indulgent, have reduced their orders. Everyone's happy. Except Victor and Paul.

Victor, after emerging from his fever-induced lethargy, realized that Gabrielle had come every day to give Jeanne a hand. He lost his temper, insisted that Jeanne change tactics. She didn't let him go on.

"That's unrealistic, Victor! I need someone out front for the customers. I haven't got your experience! I can't do everything. Why are you so hostile about Gabrielle giving me a hand?"

Victor coughs a little, short of breath. He has to come up with an intelligent answer.

"I don't like customers intruding in my business."

"That's no reason. Your bakery is open because, thanks to Gabrielle, I can bake your bread in peace. And dammit, if you could see her you'd realize she's not the one doing the favour, you are. She feels useful, she finally has something to do to fill her days. In fact, you should think about keeping her on when you're better. Gabrielle would help you strictly out of friendship, like me."

"I don't give a shit about friendship. Just make sure she never comes up here."

He turns his back on Jeanne. He doesn't have the upper hand. He has no choice.

Those harsh words, the fear in Victor's voice, unknown till now. Another way of being together.

((

Jeanne is home again. At night, worn out after her day at the bakery, she spends a few hours on her translation. She has no choice: the deadline, marked prominently on the calendar, is a constant reminder. Paul isn't happy either. With himself most of all. And with the way things get away from him. Victor and Gabrielle cast their nets wide. Paul doesn't mind being pushed into a corner by his sister, if it makes her happy; for her he's willing to step aside, but not for Victor. What particularly offends him is that his rage now has an object, making him feel obliged to fight a man he thinks of as a loser without really knowing why, most likely because popular wisdom in this village has so decided; he's just following the herd. As long as he was subject to his fits of temper but didn't know the cause, he was a hero. Martyr to a fate he hadn't chosen. An inevitability. A destiny. But ever since his anger has taken the form of a woman's body, absent from his nights, ever since it has imprinted on him the image of Jeanne bending over Victor's body, without desire and without threat, he's the one who's a loser. And in front of Jeanne, who is overworked, fulfilled by the presence of those she loves — who include him, he's sure of that — he feels even more enraged, even more a loser.

Victor is doing better. A caged animal. He wants Jeanne to buy him a bottle of gin. She lies to him. Declares, even swears that the food she brings comes from her kitchen, not the Germains'. The days Gabrielle doesn't come to the bakery — when her body decides for her — he mellows. It's as if sickness has stripped him, has removed a protective coat of varnish. Jeanne goes upstairs to him after she closes the bakery. He tells her again that she's working too hard, that she's the one who is paying for his sins. That it isn't fair. His face is drawn, sickness has aged him all at once. She asked him, "What sins, Victor?"

He replied without hesitation, mischievously, as if he were playing with words again.

"Why the sin of living, sweetie, the sin of living."

☾

Victor, Paul, Gabrielle: three persons in one, the blessed Trinity, a mystery, a revealed truth that can't be comprehended through Christian doctrine. To each his wound. Gabrielle's, at least, Jeanne can imagine. The young woman has nothing to hide. An open book. A book with simple words: a night in July, an automobile. Muscles, nerves, bones: devastated. In her head, fear is permanent. One can come close to that wound, meet it head-on, fight it at times. The truth revealed by the mystery of that wound carries far and wide, well beyond pity or compassion. It is something like love, that's the mystery we can't understand.

But Paul and Victor. Their wound like a torrent, or the wind. Enigmatic. Paul, his inability to name it, Victor, his refusal to talk about it or his irony that masks it. What reckless driver has struck them, them too, one night in July along a deserted road?

Jeanne has no particular fondness for mysteries. Or for the Trinity or the Redemption. She is not a believer. Hasn't changed, is just a little older. Is no more ambitious than before. Wants to exist — only that. She has taken on a life in which it is only possible to exist in relation to injuries that aren't even hers. But not believing doesn't stop anyone from baking bread, from demanding her share of caresses from other beings, from offering her warmth as well. And so, perhaps, at a bend in the path, the landscape will be revealed, grandiose, as soothing as an offering.

☾

That life has gone on for nearly two months, long enough to get through the winter. Victor is back on the job after four or five weeks, a few hours a day at first, then little by little Jeanne loses her title baker-in-chief and the pleasure that goes with the office. He is still tired, irritable. Which she interprets as sadness. He hasn't pardoned Gabrielle's presence. He is constantly apologizing for his bad temper. Jeanne tells herself that it really is time to go back to her translation and to Paul, who's no more lovable than Victor nowadays, except that he doesn't apologize.

She is working twice as hard. The translation deadline is coming dramatically closer. She's working on the veranda again, with a space-heater at her feet. Spring is timidly settling in, in the clearing the snow is slow to melt. She opens her eyes wide: it's the only season in this part of the country that she hasn't yet seen burst open. Soon it will be a year since she arrived; she'll have experienced them all, will have known the first poignant savours, known the heat and cold, the silence and noise. Will they award her a certificate as landed immigrant for the occasion? Is one year long enough to acquire a nationality?

6

*T*he cold night in the clearing. Is there an animal in this forest that is concerned about his absence? An old friend, a rival, a mate? Or perhaps his disappearance won't have made any difference. Every rustle, every cry, every flowing stream will go on without him. Without memory. Does he guess at the presence of this woman who has taken refuge in her images?

Jeanne is reassured: when you disappear, in one way or another you go on living. Marianne is proof of that. She has never been lost. Has always been close at hand. The years have flown by for her, too. She is discreet now, as if she loves Jeanne enough to let her have all the space. She's still radiant. Small wrinkles have appeared at the corners of her eyes, like

Jeanne's; her long hair, her body, her graceful movements haven't changed in eighteen years. She is happy. Has always been the one to leave behind those who orbited around her. Has arranged to be the one who has the most weight. Has never had the sense of being nothing or no one, sitting in a deserted railway station, at the back of a café, or on a freshly painted veranda.

Too bad if the images lie, thinks Jeanne.

She is beginning to struggle against sleep. Holds the cognac against her chest, drinks it straight from the bottle. The way Paul drinks his beer or Victor his green bottles of gin with the label in the shape of a heart.

And too bad if those we love lie, she thinks again.

SIXTH STRAY BULLET

*O*nce the translation is done, Jeanne hasn't got any others. No matter what doors she knocks on, she's told: "Come back in the fall. Things slow down in the summer."

The veranda has become a cage, the clearing a pen. In this place either you move around relentlessly like Paul and Victor, with work making up for everything that's lacking here, that elsewhere would be called the pulse of life, the frenzy, the frantic rhythm of the world, or you have to go away to get them back.

On Thursdays she joins Victor at the bakery. One or two afternoons a week she devotes to Gabrielle. The rest of the time: emptiness and silence. No, thinks Jeanne, I'm not the one going around in circles like an idiot, no, there's a mistake, that's not what I chose, it doesn't match the picture in the catalogue. The time to fill between Gabrielle's anxieties, Victor's bread, and Paul's caresses. That time could be blessed if she knew how to do something with it. The images no longer help; if only there were one buried away somewhere, that would give her something to do with her hands, her arms, her head while she waits for a new translation job, some surprise, some disaster that would land on her and remind her that of time, there is never enough.

Jeanne finally takes refuge on the veranda with the collected poems of René Char, the Pléiade edition. A precious copy that she couldn't bring herself to return to the university library. The only misdemeanour in her life. She spends days at a time reading, learning by heart poems that, come Thursday, she recites to Victor. Who listens reverently, his hands in the dough, even if it's clear that geography interests him more than poetry.

☾

Jeanne moves on from the Trinity to a quartet. René Char becomes the man most present, most fervent in her life that summer. Wherever she goes he goes with her. His words become the path that she takes through the forest to the river, the fragile light between the trees and the living water on the rocks. His words become Victor's nervous gaze, Gabrielle's limping gait, Paul's closed face. But most of all, his words become Jeanne's doubts, as sturdy as her convictions. Because she's well aware that the poems of René Char can never bring back her life as it was before, with its plans, its promises, its agitation. Jeanne as literary translator, no doubt she'll have to forget about. Reality is the bare clearing before her, the mountains, the harsh beauty of this region, its silence and its remoteness. Its ability to close itself around beings like a trap. A vise. There will be a price to pay. You cannot exist everywhere at once. The portion of heaven that has been allotted to each of us contains only a minute quantity of stars, even if, on certain nights, their number provokes such vertigo that it could make you sick.

Towards the end of summer Jeanne emerges from her lair. Gabrielle's episodic sadness brings her to the village nearly every day. She leaves René Char behind. Relieved. She is needed. Life is making claims on her to do jobs whose necessity and simplicity cannot be measured against any poem.

☾

She wishes she could convince herself that this feeling of uselessness is only due to the absence of work. But there's also Paul, closed away inside his shell, his despair disguised as anger, his abrupt movements, his impatience, his skill at never focussing on Jeanne, the absolute power of attraction that drives her towards him; but the darts, constant, whistling past on their way to destroying whatever tries to endure between them; the darts — a threat hanging over all her images.

Her disappointment. In the end, he is the person most remote from her. She knew in advance. Said yes all the same. Lucidity is not exempt from hope.

Jeanne is becoming very familiar with Paul's tactics. When the tension mounts too high, when he embodies only anger, in order to break nothing, to lose nothing of what he gets from her, he shifts his rage onto something indisputable. Almost invariably onto Gabrielle's accident or, rather, onto whoever caused it. And then even though it's unbearable, no one can reproach him for that rage.

Paul can talk only when the subject is his sister. And propped up by a case of twenty-four. Amazingly, he can go on for hours. Jeanne listens to him religiously, watching for the inconsistency that will reveal the anger beneath the anger, the nameless one, deafening, yet without echo. For Paul, on the one hand there is Gabrielle, broken, fragile, unhappy. Captive in her body and her head. Hobbled. Divested of her dreams and of her life. Reduced to pathetic gestures. Dependent. On the other hand, there's someone out there carrying on as if nothing had happened, someone who may not even know what he has done, thinking he'd struck a deer or some other animal; he breathes, laughs, loves in the most total innocence. He gets behind the wheel when he's been drinking, telling himself this road is always deserted. It may be one of the forest workers Paul pays every week, or one of the farmers who pay him for saving the life of a sickly calf or a cow. Or one of those young men who one day run into Gabrielle in the village or somewhere else and, looking her up and down, think what a shame, such a pretty girl, then continue along their way. Or it could just as well be a stranger, someone who was on that road for the first time simply by chance and hasn't come back. Whatever the case, the whole world is contained in the body of that enemy, as if to explain the extent of Paul's determination.

What's most unbearable for him is imagining that on the fateful night, someone saw the signs of that young woman dressed in pale colours. At the last second, a bad reflex made the car swerve. He hit Gabrielle. He'd slowed down just after the impact, but immediately his foot, stepping on the gas, determined what would happen next. He goes on living, like the forest worker or the farmer, sure that he's hit an animal: he breathes, laughs, loves. But somewhere in his memory he knows, all the time. Whatever scenario Paul works out, the guiltiest, the most tormented individual is always him. Never the reckless driver. At first Jeanne tried to be reassuring, tried to make him understand that all assumptions were pointless. It might not have made any dif-ference if Gabrielle had been found right away. The damage was no doubt already irreversible. He had to stop fanning those flames. In fact she tried to tell him: "Get rid of that anger and all the rest of your rage; I'm not sure I can stay in the eye of the hurricane much longer." A waste of breath. That very real injury serves as a pretext for other injuries, other wounds. Jeanne has no idea how many there are hiding in a cluster behind the shield that is Gabrielle, or if there is only the one holding that shield at the level of his heart, and if it has no other face than Paul's.

She has to agree that up to a point, Paul is right. Living close to Gabrielle means living in the shadow of the person who caused the tragedy. The young woman's hesitant gait, her pain, her fatigue, her trembling, her crying fits preclude forgetting. But there's only Paul who can fight with the phantom, howling, "Who? Who?" and understand that the blows he inflicts on the air come back right in his face.

Jeanne hasn't confided in Gabrielle — for obvious reasons — or in Victor about these long monologues of Paul's that regularly prove his inability to live outside the anger that consumes him, that he holds back and subdues, just as a tracked animal subdues its fear at every crackling sound in the forest. She has revealed nothing, because on the day when she hears her own voice name that anger, all the other words she uses to describe the ties that attach her to Paul will be reduced to nothingness.

☾

One evening, Paul's father knocks timidly on their door. Jeanne is fond of him, this gentle man so different from his son, who is growing old with the sorrow of seeing his daughter, possessed of the greatest gift for life, restricted to a series of solitary and insignificant gestures, the anti-thesis to the high hopes she'd once had. He has come to tell them that a distant relative has died, that he and his wife want to attend the funeral, that they'd like to see that branch of the family, expatriated twenty-five years ago, at the other end of the province. He explains sheepishly, as if he were already pleading guilty to an accusation yet to be levelled, that it would be good for them to have a break, to see people and, he adds with a sigh, to be away from Gabrielle so they could recharge their batteries. It isn't easy to support her, to be equal to the task, to guess what they should or shouldn't do. For some time now, they haven't known how to deal with her. He falls silent and looks down. Seems terribly ill at ease.

"We may not be the best parents for her under the circumstances ..."

"There's no problem," replies Paul, "Gabrielle will come here while you're away."

He smiles sadly.

"I know, I can count on you. But don't let her think we want her taken care of like a child. I wouldn't want to humiliate her. If she says no, we won't go."

"Go in peace, leave everything to us."

Paul sees his father to the car. Jeanne watches them from the veranda, side by side, leaning against the car with their arms crossed, talking without looking at one another. It's getting dark. A group of nervous and harried birds fly back to the forest.

Paul doesn't come inside right away after his father leaves. He fusses around outside, in the garage. Half an hour later, he comes back to Jeanne. Very calm. In a translator's reflex, she tries to find the precise term to describe him. Placated, that's the word she's looking for. An unusual match with Paul's skin. As his parents want to leave the next morning, they try to work out the best strategy to avoid hurting Gabrielle. They agree on a scenario. Just present matters to her cleverly, without lying. She won't try to stand up to her brother. Out of affection more than submission.

"One day not so far away," Paul begins, "my parents will be too old or simply won't be there to look after Gabrielle. She'll live with us permanently. It's in the nature of things."

The statements have come out of his mouth with all the assurance of a tree in its immobility. After that he tips his head and knocks back half a beer.

The thunderbolt has just landed in the middle of the table that separates them. Jeanne stares at him, taken aback. Gabrielle's future, predictable, is something they've all thought about but never mentioned. Each of them — including the person principally concerned — knows that it's around this obvious fact that life will be organized. Each takes from this projection the small truth that allows him to breathe more easily: the parents are reassured, they can grow old now without that anxiety, Paul's sense of guilt finds in that arrangement its forgiveness.

But Jeanne's future. He has declared: "She'll live with us." He has seen far ahead, has embraced all of life, and that included Jeanne. It's the first time he has mentioned the future. As well, tonight he's amazingly calm. So that's what life will be like? Only a few beings who are not at ease with themselves or with their words, who will give her the perfect and imperfect measure of love? So that's what life will be like? A bakery, an isolated white house, another at the edge of the village with a vast garden behind it? That's what her existence will be her whole life through. The world on a small scale?

Jeanne, in silence, goes on staring at Paul, who doesn't know how to interpret the scene. Is it the prospect of taking charge of Gabrielle that unsettles her, or is there something else that he hasn't grasped yet?

So that's what life will be like? Images to Jeanne's rescue: elsewhere, congested roads, jam-packed airports, stadiums full to bursting, shuttles heading into space, double heart-and-lung transplants, high-speed trains, the stock market, the silhouette of René Char in 1944, hurrying at midnight down a dark street in the south of France, turning around frequently to be sure that he's not being followed, and hiding in his overcoat the coded instructions for the next operation by his cell of Resistance fighters. Life.

He said "we," she keeps telling herself quick as a flash, he said "when my parents aren't there any more." Meaning: "Ten, fifteen, twenty years from now we'll be together. You and me. The three of us." If he took rings from his pocket that they would then slip onto one another's fingers, it wouldn't surprise her. How can a person say "yes" with such fervour and at the same time howl "no?"

Finally, Paul realizes what is troubling her. He's talked too much, that'll teach him. You have to watch out. He can hear very distinctly the intensity of the "yes" and "no" that Jeanne, through the sudden pallor of her face and that phoney knowing look, is offering him by way of a response to what he has just declared.

She read in *National Geographic* that Everest can't be conquered in one stage, not even under the best conditions. You have to become acclimatized. Climb up a little and go back down. Climb up again from one camp to the next. Spend the night there, uncomfortable, with breathing difficult, sleep impossible. To increase the red corpuscles in the blood, to accustom the body so it can function at a higher altitude.

Then go back down the next morning, the better to climb up again later; That's what explorers are not shown — the hesitation, the body's resistance, its vulnerability when life becomes too vast, and the air thinner. They dangle the conquest, the summit awarded like a gift after the ascent. But not the nature or consequences of the effort. That night, holding each other tightly in their bed, Jeanne and Paul, unable to sleep, wonder if they have enough red corpuscles to continue the ascent.

The next day, at the end of the afternoon, Paul brings Gabrielle to their house. Jeanne has pulled the garden table into the middle of the clearing, covered it with a red-checked cloth and laden it with food. A party, a picnic. A carefree pause in the summer heat. A way of telling them that today she's there with them, entirely, that her arms are open wide, that she won't hesitate to close them and embrace their anger or their suffering, if that is their desire. Let them enjoy it now. The three of them around the table, light, contented, as they were a year ago when Jeanne came into their lives and the three of them, for the duration of a summer, believed that love was a definitive refuge.

They've drunk wine and beer. Gabrielle tries to persuade Jeanne to make a garden in the area where they're sitting. A big round garden, fenced-in English style to keep out wild hares. She cuts it into triangles, arranging the vegetables and flowers as in a French garden. Gabrielle, cheeks red, eyes shining from the wine.

"A wonderful project," she says.

It's already her garden. Jeanne sees herself later with Gabrielle, lost somewhere on the line to the future, here in a fenced-in garden, more modest and not as round as the one she describes, but quite real. Her new images. Those of the future. Larger than life.

Gabrielle has no illusions about what lies ahead for her. The images of her future she has long since drawn, sometimes with dread, sometimes with lucidity. The most distressing have finally built a nest for themselves where it's warm. She bears them sometimes like a cross, sometimes like a second skin. She's not in a crucifixion mood tonight. Yes, the garden will be here, exactly where she described it.

At the end of the evening, at the moment when each of them in silence is busy clearing the table, Gabrielle tells the others point-blank: "Anyway, my biggest regret is the fact that I'll never have children, never have a family of my own."

Instinctively, Jeanne approaches her to deal with her distress and the tears that will come. But her friend goes on stacking glasses and plates. Shrugs.

"That's life! You mustn't worry about me."

Jeanne takes the tray and they go inside, while above them

thousands of blind and silent stars preside over the first night of the world, as usual.

Gabrielle has gone upstairs. Jeanne drains the bottles while she finishes tidying up the kitchen with Paul, who is acting impatient again, chain-smoking, and knocking back beer after beer. She keeps hearing Gabrielle express her regrets. And as she repeats them to herself, she imagines a child. First one cell, then two, then a small indistinct mass until the joyful body of a small child appears in the clearing. Her child. Gabrielle's. She turns around, intrigued by the sudden stillness and silence of Paul at her side: he is watching her with unprecedented vigilance, he sees not her but the child who is running in the clearing and has just escaped to the edge of the forest.

((

Jeanne's pregnancy. For nine months the object of everyone's attention. Gabrielle, who has dusted off her textbooks on child care and obstetrics, makes sure she has detailed knowledge of every stage of her condition. Paul keeps his mood swings to himself, agrees with all of his sister's observations and advice, backing them up by drawing parallels between human and bovine gestation. Jeanne sometimes thinks that her pregnancy is really about the relationship between Paul and Gabrielle.

As for Victor, he's sure it will be a boy. He makes the most of these months, as if they were his final ones with Jeanne. Often when she is forming loaves of bread, he comes up behind her, puts his arms around her, hands flat on her belly. They stay like that, unmoving, Victor's chin resting on Jeanne's shoulder, waiting for the baby to display his presence by kicking, which fascinates him.

"If Paul could see me now!"

They laugh, it's true that they make an odd couple. Welded together.

"Are you happy, Jeanne?" he whispers in her ear one morning near the end of her pregnancy, when she has rushed to join him at the oven so he can feel her belly contract; the first signs of what lies ahead in a few weeks time.

Happy? Pregnancy is a respite. A victory over the future. The victory of the body that is only working to construct the present: tissues, bones, blood. As if the amount of oxygen available were enough, were making it possible to continue the ascent without being constantly obsessed with the next breath.

☾

The child. One hot and humid July night, similar to Gabrielle's pitch black night. The stars, Jeanne's controlled breathing, Paul who drives fast and says every five minutes that they'll soon be there. If it's a girl, she'll be called Marianne. The final effort, the rending, the summit, the end: never again Jeanne and Marianne, never again Jeanne and Paul or Jeanne and Victor or Jeanne and Gabrielle. They'll have to place the name of a child between them.

At noon, exhaustion. Outside, scorching heat. The name will be not Marianne but Jérôme. A nurse lays him in his mother's arms. Then Paul takes him, the child fits in his hands. An emotion that sweeps everything away.

He has promised — she insisted — that he'd drop in on Victor to tell him about the birth of their son after he's told his parents. It's late, the stairways are dark. He keeps his promise. It's the first time he's gone up to Victor's place — and the last, he tells himself. The door is wide open, Victor is in the kitchen, fixing something to eat.

They stand there, the two of them, face to face. Paul has reeled off his news in one sentence. Victor asks about Jeanne. Paul could have stepped in past the threshold, Victor could have offered him a beer. Paul has gone again. Without saying goodbye.

☾

Very quickly after his birth, Jérôme showed Jeanne that he'd already chosen sides. As soon as his eyes stopped being slightly hazy blue marbles incapable of focussing on an object, as soon as his gaze was able to make out what would connect him to the world, what his first food would be, he hasn't looked away. Paul could become any father, from the most indifferent to the most loving. Jérôme had chosen him — him and him alone. Jeanne and Gabrielle would be angels, affectionate, caring, both on the same footing. The places on the chessboard had been distributed once and for all.

That's fine, thinks Jeanne, it gives the child a family that's out of the ordinary; the four of them won't be like anything conventional, won't have to adapt to any model, will stick together. Later on, they won't reproach themselves for open sores, for badly healed wounds, the way most families do. They'll lick them, each on his own, of course, in a corner, but they won't move away from one another because they'll have the same ones, in the same places on their bodies. Maybe it will be like that. With a little luck.

For the time being, mission accomplished. The road has been mapped out. Gabrielle has what she wanted. She lives half the time with Paul and Jeanne. Jérôme is a colicky baby; she knows what to do. The grandparents come nearly every day, they don't want to miss a thing. The only cloud on the horizon: Victor isn't part of the handsome family portrait. Much more than a cloud for Jeanne. An emptiness, a desertion.

Shortly after Jérôme's birth, Jeanne goes back to the bakery on Thursdays. She lets Victor know that she could come more often. It's tempting not to be always a mother when there's another who wants nothing more, tempting to take one's distance from the explorers in order to be alone with another sherpa.

Victor couldn't ask for anything more. But he warns Jeanne never to reserve a place for him, no matter how hypothetical, in the family photo. In plain language, that means: "I love you, but not the rest of them, and your son is part of the rest of them." Jérôme will come to the bakery frequently during his childhood, will feel comfortable there. Victor will be nice to him but he'll keep his distance. Jérôme will be intrigued by Victor. A world apart, a mysterious world, of which his mother knows all the secrets. Such familiarity between him and her.

Life goes on. People are surprised to see Jeanne working so hard at the bakery. Despite her life with Jérôme. While Paul knows that another photo exists, a photo of Victor and Jeanne in the bakery, smiling. A photo that nothing will be able to tear. Especially not him. A photo he could have got along without.

7

*P*ropped up on cushions and wrapped in her blanket, Jeanne does not move. She'd just have to lean over slightly and reach out her arm and she could pick up the flashlight. She doesn't want to know if the moose is still alive. She's afraid that the worst is yet to come and that it won't be an easy death. Groans, convulsions, suffering that drags on and on.

If only she could let sleep overcome her. At dawn she would open her eyes and the clearing would appear, pale and nude with its sparse yellow hay and its nearly symmetrical scattering of rocky islands. He would no longer be lying in the middle of the clearing, he would have vanished with the night. She would get up, her back and neck aching. She'd go outside. The early hours of the day would be cold and damp.

She would peer around the vicinity carefully. He would have disappeared. She would no longer know if she had dreamed. No longer know the difference between the things that have happened, those that are happening, and those that will happen. She would stand in the middle of the clearing, and her anguish, too, would have vanished with the night.

SEVENTH STRAY BULLET

*L*ife goes on. Without Jeanne's knowing why or how, the clocks race out of control. It's not like a book to translate; she doesn't spend long hours struggling over a page or a chapter. She has to deal with what is most urgent. Even René Char is asleep for all eternity beneath the trees on one of the small wooded islands in the River Sorgue. Finished too the aerial drifting above parks, forests, rivers. Most often, the breathlessness of the coyote that runs at night through the beacon lights.

☾

Euphoria is in the past. The child is still the daily miracle in their lives. But you get used to miracles that heal only temporarily. In fact, they don't heal everything, don't fill a lifetime, the empty zones stay empty and each person begins again the task of filling them on his own.

Jeanne has been crossed off the list of those who might have offered her translation work. Her last frantic attempts have been in vain.

"Jeanne who? You live where?"

Out of the loop, away from well-read and cosmopolitan civilization, there's no salvation.

New pains have appeared in Gabrielle's leg. "Degeneration," the doctors have diagnosed, a long-term consequence of the damage caused by the accident. Nothing shows except that her limp is a little more pronounced and she grimaces when she bends over Jérôme.

Paul, his two-headed work, and his family. His profound anger, which he carries on his shoulders the way he carries Jérôme, to make him laugh, and the certainty now that it won't cost him what he most cares about.

It's neither disenchantment nor bitterness. Only the moment when the child — who has always dreamed over photos of Everest — departs the explorer's body, leaving him alone, without illusions, with the icy winds, the lack of oxygen, the material to transport.

Paul's moods are harder to put up with. Because of Jérôme, because of the world of naïveté and unconcern to which he's brought them. He worships his father, deploys all kinds of tactics and strategies to get his attention. It works. Charisma is hereditary, Jeanne thinks. But she's afraid that Jérôme will take his father's anger and place it prominently on his little chest. A badge, a sign of belonging.

Maybe Paul's rage has finally contaminated Jeanne. She's resentful because she doesn't have access to that anger. Because he stays behind a closed door. Alone, flayed. Because throughout the time she has known him, she hasn't stopped striking out. Her reddened fist. Nothing. No answer. Silence, always, always.

☾

A Sunday morning. The sun. Reassuring aromas: coffee, Victor's bread. Jérôme is playing on the veranda. Now he feels that the house is too cramped. She keeps an eye on him from the kitchen. He arranges objects around him, shifts them, stacks them. He builds, organizes. A territory, a fortress. In his mind, an image he embodies by the way he moves. Could it be that images are hereditary too?

Nothing has fated this morning for a crisis. Paul has slept in. When he comes down to the kitchen he doesn't let himself be caught up by the lightness around him. His heavy movements. Everything he touches, too. His impatience expressed through familiar sounds amplified: coffee-pot banged onto the table, fridge door slammed. A customary attitude, a Sunday like any other. He is absorbed in his mail, which he hasn't looked at in days. On the veranda, Jérôme is savouring his conquest of Everest. A pile of saucepans he's been trying to keep in place for more than fifteen minutes. Paul glances furtively at Jeanne across from him. His anger, his chaos.

She protests. No, not this morning, not this anger again. It's not the first time she has expressed her exasperation to him, but this time, in her voice and in her words, there's something new, something resolutely foreign to Jeanne, something that tries to wound, and succeeds.

He gets up so suddenly that he knocks over his chair. Jérôme is startled. The saucepans come crashing down. Paul races up the stairs four at a time. The child is on the verge of tears. Paul comes back down with a few things. The veranda door slams. Jeanne will have her peaceful Sunday.

It lasts for three days, Jeanne's peaceful Sunday. Paul comes back on Tuesday late in the day. His anger gone.

Every explorer holds on to his pride during the difficult passages. Especially when he transforms himself into a warrior. Jeanne asks for no explanations. He ran away, did he? Water off a duck's back.

A lie. She waited for him the first night. Didn't give in to sleep until dawn, when she realized he wouldn't be coming back. Then, shortly afterwards, Jérôme's high little voice woke her up: "Papa! Papa!"

Paul wasn't in the bed beside his mother. She dressed him quickly, took him to his grandparents. Smiling, stoical. Until she'd closed the bakery door behind her.

Jeanne rooted there, surrounded by the hot bread. Her tears. Victor finally puzzled out the reason through sentences she didn't finish. At the end of the day, at gin time, he took her up to his place. He had grand theories. To Jeanne's surprise, he took Paul's side.

"It takes cunning," he told her, "to live with someone who has an understanding of love. Paul aimed right. He let fly the only dart that could wound you."

She hates the word "runaway." A reaction to rigid authority, associated with adolescence. Paul is nothing like an adolescent; Jeanne doesn't represent any form of authority. She prefers the word "absence." Paul's absence, the absence of his love, of his anger too. The absence of Jérôme's father, of Gabrielle's brother. The absence of the veterinarian that she must try, awkwardly, to explain to the farmers who call, the absence of the boss of the forest workers who show up at the house. Paul's absences, rather. Because after the first there will be others. Like memory lapses, black holes in space, bullet holes in the centre of a target.

Paul's absences, now recurrent. That respond undeniably to the same scenario: an inner tension that rises, that he tries to suppress, that then triumphs over him. And just when the dike gives way, he disappears. Returns some days later. Liberated. Until next time. After a number of absences Jeanne tells him that he's managed to get to her, that she doesn't understand why he persists in wanting to hurt her; what's she supposed to tell Jérôme, whose questions one day will go beyond the stage of, "Where papa?" and get sharper? The humiliation he will read in his mother's eyes. She appears strong and detached as she lets it all out, but one question consumes her. She can't hide her helplessness when she asks him where he goes every time and, even more, with whom, that allows him come back so relieved.

For the sleepless nights alone in her bed have now undertaken to provide her with images. Insistent, devastating. The village, the main street deserted at ten p.m. A girl sitting on the edge of the sidewalk, her hair a mess, her skin-tight jeans, her boots, her bracelets, her cigarette. Paul's truck appears at the end of the street and slows down when it comes to the young woman. Who gets up, smiling, and mockingly looks Jeanne squarely in the eyes just before she opens the door. The revelation: Marianne's face, unmistakably.

And so Marianne is back in her life, after years of staying in the background, keeping quiet, stepping aside, years of letting her have all the space she needs by giving her the impression that she'd finally arrived, the proof being that

Jeanne no longer needed her. Marianne comes back as a rival, a witch, she's taken on the appearance of the girls you see in the village during the summer next to the guys' motorcycles, and in the winter next to their Ski-Doos.

When Jeanne tries to drive that image away it strikes again, more powerfully: Marianne's voice, her delicate skin, Paul's laugh, his muscular body. But even more than seeing them together, what drives her to despair is seeing them united against her so that she'll finally learn what she has never known: how to hate those she loves. She'll never be forgiven then for her lack of excess, her way of grasping feelings by the middle rather than by their extremes, her fondness for fires that smoulder rather than those that consume everything in their path.

"But you don't get it, Jeanne, you really don't get it!" replies Paul. "I'm not going after you, I'm sparing you, you and Jérôme."

Is he lying? she wonders. The first sign of exhaustion? An equipment breakdown? A moment's inattention? An oxygen bottle that's fallen into space? The ascent called into question.

As if he were reading her mind, Paul has come up to her: "I've never lied, don't ask me questions, let me have that space."

The tone more that of prayer than of an order. With his hand in Jeanne's hair — such an ordinary gesture — and on his face the fleeting expression he wears now and then, which resembles despair when the situation demands too much of him: too much confidence, too much simplicity.

Jérôme has started screaming and pulling at his father's jeans. He's hungry. He's reminding them that he is the third player, the way out par excellence, the portion of love that's intact. Paul picks him up and takes him to the kitchen. Jérôme has switched from screaming to laughing. Jeanne watches them move away. A twosome. "We won't have any more children," she promises herself. The night lessons of blonde Marianne and Paul are starting to bear fruit.

Paul's absences have become her wounds. Jeanne anticipates them, dreads them. One morning, between customers, Victor tells her: "You're too perfect, it was just a matter of time until you joined the ranks of the sickly. Welcome aboard!"

8

In a few minutes, the first light of dawn will appear. Jeanne has dozed off with the bottle of cognac beside her. Hasn't left her post. She's asleep now with her cheek against the cold damp glass of a veranda window. The moose has been dead for hours without her knowing, she didn't hear the muffled sound the animal made when he slipped into the forest where he was born.

When Jeanne wakes up she'll feel cheated. Annoyed with herself. Will tell herself that last night was the reflection of the past years: she thought she was so vigilant when she was actually asleep, always that imbalance between that which existed and that which she wanted to exist. She reacted the

way everyone reacts in such cases: she chose her own version
of reality.

Dawn. A truck is speeding along the road. In her sleep,
Jeanne hears distinctly the rumbling of the motor. Her brain
transforms the sound into an image, she is dreaming: the
truck isn't a truck now, but an easily identifiable car that's
driving towards the house, then comes to a halt at the veranda,
two police officers get out, Jeanne goes to meet them.

"Are you the spouse of Paul Germain?"

EIGHTH STRAY BULLET

*L*ife goes on. From the height of his eleven years, Jérôme is racing towards adolescence. In the village people go into raptures over his physique, say he'll be a strapping young man. His father's son. He wants to be a veterinarian. Whenever he can, he goes along when Paul gets a call from a farmer. What he prefers: the complicated cases, the emergencies. His father's son.

Life goes on. Paul, unchanged. His big, upright, muscular body defying his inner squalls, his faded jeans, his absences, his silences. But his grey temples, his hair that he now wears short. The grey that accentuates the physical resemblance between him and Gabrielle, whose totally grey hair makes her look older than her brother, though he's ten years her senior. Life goes on. The Germain clan: Paul, Gabrielle, Jérôme. And the parents, so old now. Jeanne is convinced that Jérôme has spared Gabrielle the worst. Teasing, she still calls her "nanny." At first, Gabrielle was embarrassed when Jeanne called her that, because the word was a perfect description of the visceral tie that had developed instantly between herself and Jérôme. She was afraid that one day Jeanne would reproach her for it. Today though she realizes that Jérôme was her gift from Jeanne, her response to fate, to misfortune, to the blind injustice of the world that had made her a prisoner. But above all, Jérôme was her response to Gabrielle's affliction, a response of love and hope. Gabrielle also knows that Paul and Jeanne have given her a life, a life with them, between them. Over time, the bitterness has been erased. There remains of course her body which gradually, constantly, is deteriorating, and the more and more opaque dark spells in her head. But gone is the rancour over that hot night in July and the lunatic driver who mowed her down. Jeanne, Paul, and Jérôme have accomplished that miracle.

Life goes on. Victor. A haven since Jeanne's arrival in this part of the country. His open arms. Her family when she became an outsider to the Germain clan again. The anguish he dragged around during all of last year. Jeanne's reproaches to herself — her lack of vigilance — concerning Victor. He has just turned fifty, can't come to terms with it but doesn't talk about it. He only mentioned to Jeanne one night, between two slugs of gin, that he was lonely, that he was no longer satisfied with what he had: the village was stifling him, young men walk out on men who are aging, and then what was the sense of those Saturday nights in town, in any case he came home alone on Sunday, sometimes the smell of bread even turned his stomach. At the slightest provocation he repeated: "What a fraud, what a fraud I am!"

Victor's new credo. He has closed himself up again, but that doesn't mean he has banished Jeanne. She felt helpless. She let things go, busy as she was keeping Paul and Jérôme close to her, as if Victor were someone she couldn't lose. She didn't know what to say, what to do in the face of his despair. One Saturday, after a particularly difficult week in the bakery — Victor having been unspeakably sad — as a last resort Jeanne brought him her stolen copy of the collected poems of René Char and told him she would have preferred to give him all her translations of *National Geographic* articles, but the words of René Char were a kind of journey too. They would help him. "Maybe," she murmured, looking away. And then she added something enormous and minute, something precious and pointless: "I love you, Victor." She left the book on the low table in the living room, between the ashtray and the bottle of gin. Victor went on staring at the TV.

☾

And suddenly, Jeanne didn't understand why, but she realized there was no more expedition, that she was alone on the trail.

It all began with an afternoon phone call two days earlier. Gabrielle asked her why the bakery had been closed since the day before. As soon as she'd hung up she looked at her watch and dialled Victor's number. No answer. She jumped in her car and headed for the village. First she had to pick up Jérôme at school and take him to his grandparents'. She slowed down in front of the bakery; the "Open Tomorrow" sign wasn't in the window.

In the car, Jérôme asked what she knew about Victor's mother.

"Who was talking about her?"

"At school they say things."

"What things?"

"About Victor."

"What things about Victor?" replied Jeanne impatiently.

"Nothing, forget it."

In a tone of voice that sounded like Paul's.

As they pulled up to his grandparents' house, Jérôme didn't want to get out when she told him she was going to Victor's, that she wouldn't be long.

"I want to go too!"

"No."

"Why not?"

"Jérôme, get out, I'll be back in a while."

He got out, slammed the door, looked at her with fire in his eyes. His father's son.

Jeanne set off for the bakery again. Jérôme didn't go inside the house. He headed in the same direction as his mother.

The door to the bakery is locked, of course. Jeanne takes the back stairs up to Victor's place. Knocks. For a long time. She's sure he is there, because the car is in the garage. She's the only person with a key to the bakery. Fear. Insane images: Victor at the end of a rope, Victor in a pool of blood. Ten breaths for a single step.

Jeanne goes back down the stairs, slips inside without a sound. Leaves the door ajar behind her. You never know. She advances slowly. Everything's been left in the lurch: the loaves of bread on the racks, other loaves, unbaked, still in their pans, gaping bags of flour. Disorder. Her heart pounds. A noise from the staircase at the back of the bakery. Heavy, hesitant sounds. Victor in the doorway, devastated, a bottle of gin in one hand, a cigarette in his mouth. He's smashed, he's just smashed, she thinks.

Delirium, confusion, racks flung to the floor. For Victor too, ten breaths, one step.

He wants her to leave. He steps forward, she steps back but doesn't leave. She tries to reason with him, to fire him up. Nothing works, not even solicitude. Victor doesn't hear anything. Says over and over: "Go away, go away, leave me alone."

His face, livid and determined.

Jeanne refuses gently, this isn't the first time she's come up against Victor drunk. Just calm him down, persuade him to go upstairs, to lie down. Leave once he's asleep, taking care to empty the bottles down the sink. This time, though, he's impervious to Jeanne's words. He wants her to disappear for good, wants the bakery, the village to disappear, also for good. His fists with which he pounds his own chest.

"Get out or I won't be able to keep quiet."

She doesn't budge.

Then he reveals to her what he's been telling her, very softly, every day for thirteen years now, what he's repeated to himself a hundred times a day for eighteen years, what makes and unmakes his life, the truth contained in every loaf he forms, in every body he touches, every photo in every issue of *National Geographic* that he looks at, in the very affection he feels for Jeanne. A sentence, a single sentence, delivered in just one breath, transports them both instantaneously onto a deserted road one hot night in July. The dust, Victor's foot on the gas, the collision, the muffled sound of the light body of a young woman against the car.

Time suspended, the silence, the roof of the world, the curve of the earth. Then the tinkling of the little bells on the door. Jérôme, who has been spying on them, runs away. He too has caught a glimpse of the roof of the world.

Jeanne hot on the heels of her son.

They can run fast, eleven-year-old boys. Faster than a woman who's just had the wind knocked out of her. If Jérôme gets there before her … Jeanne can already see him, red-faced, breathless, rushing into the kitchen in front of Gabrielle: "It's Victor! It's Victor!" But it isn't his aunt he's looking for, she's not the one he has to tell, he's perfectly aware of that. At this time of day he won't find the person he's looking for, it's pointless for him to race like a hare on the run. And so he lets the voice behind him, which is calling his name non-stop, catch up with him. They're at the cemetery, Jeanne grabs him by the arm and leads him down the grey paths. She is leaning against a tree, he's sitting on a tombstone, his fingers scratching at the green moss growing over it. Only their gasping breath, only the sound of leaves swept by the wind. And for Jeanne, the superhuman effort to pull herself together. A few minutes later, she tells him it would be best if they went home. They have to walk to the car which is parked in front of the bakery. Jeanne tries to hold her son's hand as if he were still the naive little boy, or as if she herself has become a little girl again, but Jérôme won't let himself be touched and shakes off his mother's hand right away. Jeanne is shaking, can't get the key in the starter. On the way home, Jérôme tries to control himself. He can't weigh the significance of what will happen next. Jeanne can't think of anything to say. She cannot excuse Victor. Or believe him. Oh, Paul's face when Jérôme tells him what he just found out. Afterwards all four of them — she, Paul, Jérôme, Victor — trapped at the summit of Everest by the storm that they didn't see coming.

Paul's truck parked next to the shed where he stores his equipment. The light in the shed. Before Jeanne has cut the motor, Jérôme is already running towards that light. The time is a quarter to six, the first snowflakes of the year are dancing above the clearing. Won't leave a trace.

Inside the house, Jeanne paces back and forth, keeps glancing at the window. Has just one desire: to phone Victor and tell him to watch out. But in her head the images are tearing each other to pieces, and the ones of Gabrielle unconscious in the ditch are trying desperately to obliterate all the others.

You don't set the table for supper on a night like that, you don't turn on the TV, you don't pack your bags, you don't throw your arms to heaven, cursing God and his millions of stars. You watch the light in the shed, which will go out in a moment, and you listen for the sound of the footsteps of a man and his son on the gravel, going back to the house.

Paul and Jérôme were alone together for more than an hour. Each one rushes for his escape hatch as soon as his eyes meet Jeanne's. One opens a beer, the other runs to his video game.

One day Victor told Jeanne that she was living with a man who had a true understanding of love. That's what he is proving to her now. He goes to Jérôme in the living room, comes back to the kitchen almost right away. He's fixing sandwiches for two. He hasn't spoken to Jeanne; if he did, she's convinced that he'd say: "Fuck off and take that shit Victor with you!" but he is silent because he's not part of the same shipwreck as Jeanne. He goes back to the living room with the sandwiches, a beer, and a coke, commandeers the second console for the game. To see who kills the most monsters. Paul is giving his full attention to Jérôme — and at the same time to Gabrielle. Victor was right, Paul does have an understanding of love. He's in the process of spinning a web around his son, of imposing on him the law of silence. Once that's done, he'll be able to deal with his own anger.

Jeanne is excluded from that pact, that love. She goes upstairs to take refuge in her room. A little later, when she hears Jérôme coming up for the night, she will go to his room, straighten the covers. They'll both be uncomfortable. She will ask him who won the game. Jérôme will tell her that Paul did.

Paul doesn't join Jeanne that night. She hears the TV. She doesn't sleep, doesn't expect him. She thinks about Victor. Around five a.m. a motor growls — Paul's van — then vanishes as he drives away.

At the table a few hours later, Jérôme's disappointment at the sight of his father's empty chair. Another of his absences. Jeanne smiles at him.

"I'll drive you to school this morning."

Life picks up again where she and Jérôme had left it the night before.

The bakery closed. She wishes so much that the car would stop outside it by itself, that the door would open, that she'd be pushed out of the vehicle and into the bakery. An image there, suddenly, before her eyes: her copy of the poems of René Char on the low table in the living room. Has Victor even opened it, leafed through it? A foreboding, a certainty: she'll never see either of them again. The car continues along its way.

She tells Jérôme she'll come back to pick him up after school. He protests. No, he's going to his grandparents; it's Friday, on Friday he sleeps in the village. She insists. No, anyway his grandfather promised he could drive the garden tractor to get the ground ready for spring. All right, Jérôme will stay. Her anguish. How to be sure he won't talk?

Jeanne's day, alone in the white house. Her hand that started to punch in Victor's number, that she didn't stop. No ringing, nothing. Silence at the other end.

Then that crazy moose that's come to die in front of her. And she who can't stop herself from keeping watch.

9

*D*ay is dawning now. A grey, dark day. Jeanne is still asleep, an unhealthy sleep that doesn't free her from her torment. The sound of a truck again. And the same dream: a car, police officers. The sound gets louder, comes near the house. She wakes up; this time it's true, she thinks. The most important thing: not to open her eyes. Then two doors slam, like bullets being fired, she jumps, her head is splitting. She opens her eyes.

Paul's van in the clearing. He and Jérôme very close to the animal. They haven't seen her. Her ridiculous position. Quick, hide the cognac, the overflowing ashtray under the table, put back the cushions. Oh, the heart that's pounding in her head like thunder.

Jeanne is outside now, sitting on the steps. She is watching. Paul, obviously, is explaining to his son the causes of the moose's death. He crouches down, points to certain parts of the body, lifts a hind leg. Jérôme lifts it in turn. After five minutes they know more about this creature than she did after watching it for eighteen hours.

Jérôme runs to the house to get the camera. He spies his mother.

"Mama! Mama!"

He's excited, eyes bright again. Paul turns towards Jeanne.

Her anxiety has melted away in one go, replaced by an immense sadness. At this time of day Gabrielle must be asleep, her pale body tucked between the covers. And Victor? There are no more images of him in her head, only the furious hammering that keeps telling her that life goes on.

Paul walks towards her slowly, hands in his pockets. Sits down beside her. Their silence. Jérôme has gone back to the animal, with the camera in one hand and a peanut butter sandwich in the other.

"I slept at my parents' place with Jérôme. It's all right, he won't talk."

His drawling voice, with no anger.

Jeanne's gaze, which takes in the clearing, the moose, the trees, the mountains. Everything in front of her is blurred.

He won't hear Jeanne's reply. It stays walled up in her head, caught in a vise. It won't leave her pale lips: Of course, Paul, of course, he'll never talk, he'll keep the secret, bury it inside himself somewhere, maybe even forget it sometimes, till the day when this secret will turn to anger that he'll quash with long periods of silence. Of course, Paul, of course I agree with you, it can't be otherwise. Don't stir up anything that belongs to the past. Protect Gabrielle. And Victor.

Then, after a moment, she says: "I want to leave here." Paul doesn't have time to find out if that wish includes or excludes him. The phone rings, she runs to answer. A call from a farmer. Immediately, Paul races to his emergency. Just before he goes, he tells her spitefully: "They can't find Victor anywhere."

FINAL STRAY BULLET

*A*fter the summit, the descent. The stage of fatigue and caution. The chest pains lessened, oxygen finally back.

Jeanne is surprised every time: from every window in this house you see a different house. Neighbours: men, women, children. Gas mowers too early on Saturday morning, clotheslines. And in the distance, but present like sentinels, the Appalachians.

Paul couldn't separate himself from the white house. Now at least Jeanne knows where he's going when he disappears. With a mock-affected look, Gabrielle talks about their "second home."

It's a big house. Without a veranda. Gabrielle grows a tiny garden in the backyard. Her bedroom is next to Jérôme's.

Jeanne teaches English to adults at the high school two nights a week.

In the village, when people run into Paul's parents they ask about Jeanne and Jérôme. Kind neighbours barricaded one of the bakery windows after branches broken by the wind shattered the glass. In the village, people buy their bread at the grocery store now. Life goes on.

One spring evening, Paul drops on the table a letter that's addressed to Jeanne, which the village post-mistress gave him, apologizing. She'd received it some time before but was waiting till she saw him again to give it to him, then had finally forgotten it on a shelf. The letter has no return address; the postmark is so pale you can't make out the name of the place it was sent from. Paul is positive it's from Victor.

When he hears Victor's name, Jérôme breaks off his conversation with Gabrielle.

An angel passes, or a demon. Only Gabrielle doesn't see it.

Jeanne takes the letter and leaves the kitchen, shrugging. Her name and her old address, written hastily. Familiar handwriting. The sound of the letter-opener slipped carefully into the envelope. The precise movements of her fingers: this letter is a treasure.

But there's no letter.

Jeanne looks, without understanding, at the small square of ivory paper, printed, that has just slipped onto her desk.

Then things start to name themselves by themselves. First, the little square of paper is a page torn out of the poems of René Char. It's been folded awkwardly into the shape of an envelope and sealed. "My stolen book!" Jeanne lets out as she scratches the tiny wax seal with her fingernail. Finally, the treasure runs into her hand: a few grams of flour.

That's all. But that flour seems so alive in the palm of her hand.

Jeanne goes back downstairs, light. Gabrielle, carefree, asks: "What's with the letter?"
"Remember Marianne? She was at school with us, she always wore a blue necklace her father'd brought her from Nepal? Well, she wrote to me."

Gabrielle, disconsolate, searches her memory but doesn't remember Marianne.

"It doesn't matter if you've forgotten," Jeanne tells her cheerfully.

Eyes fixed on Paul, who doesn't believe her.

189